T0120968

THE
STRANGER
FROM THE
SEA

E. THORNTON GOODE, JR.

THE STRANGER FROM THE SEA

iUniverse books may be ordered through booksellers or by contacting:

iUniverse
1663 Liberty Drive
Bloomington, IN 47403
www.iuniverse.com
844-349-9409

Because of the dynamic nature of the Internet, any web addresses or links contained in this book may have changed since publication and may no longer be valid. The views expressed in this work are solely those of the author and do not necessarily reflect the views of the publisher, and the publisher hereby disclaims any responsibility for them.

Any people depicted in stock imagery provided by Getty Images are models, and such images are being used for illustrative purposes only. Certain stock imagery © Getty Images.

ISBN: 978-1-6632-2971-7 (sc)
ISBN: 978-1-6632-2972-4 (e)

Library of Congress Control Number: 2021920252

Print information available on the last page.

iUniverse rev. date: 09/28/2021

In Appreciation

I would like to thank my good friend, Galen Berry, for the use of his picture to show the reader the appearance of the character, Nick, in the story. Nick is somewhat of a cut-up and an outspoken prankster, too. Galen was a godsend, helping with proofreading and editing. He brought several things to my attention that were quite significant. Many thanks, my Friend.

My friend, Doug Carlton, has let me use his picture, so the reader may see the image of the character, Togar. Doug was also very helpful in proofreading and editing. Many thanks to you, my Friend.

I want to thank my friend, Julian Green, for letting me use his pictures here, so the reader can get an idea what the character of Tristan looks like. Julian, I gratefully appreciate it. I love you and I miss you very much. It's not fair that you should go before me.

Julian, you were such a kind, caring, loving and handsome man. When Dan passed away, I thought Julian would come here and we would share our golden years together. Julian was coming here after he retired in June of 2018. But it wasn't meant to be. He passed away on Christmas Day, 2017.

Biographical Information

Living on the SW coast of Mexico has been terrific. I've had time to do more writing and this place has actually inspired this storyline. So far, there are a total of thirteen novels. This will be the fifth one in print. Hopefully, number six will be to press soon. I also have a group of short stories I have considered putting in print as a collection. It's a possibility. We shall see.

Someone asked me where I get my ideas for stories. Strangely enough, my life experiences have had a big influence on many of them. I just hope I can get all the ones already written in print before I drop dead. GRIN!

Yes. The COVID pandemic has allowed me to complete the draft of the most recent novel, <u>The Legend of Cavenaugh Island</u>. I have spent much time writing. It still needs a lot of work. There are several others standing in line in front of it to get published. After this one, probably <u>The Seashell</u> will go to print next.

If you are unaware, here are the novels already in print. Check them out.

<u>The Old Lighthouse</u> Published in December 2007
<u>The 2</u> Published in January 2012
<u>Two Portraits in Oil</u> Published in February 2020
<u>Muraroot</u> Published in April 2021.

The first two novels are available online from buybooksontheweb.com. The second two are available from iUniverse.com.

I love it here in Mexico. I could not have chosen a better place to retire. The peace and quiet, the sound of the ocean crashing on the rocks and the cool breeze off the water are just a few things that make me smile.

I do miss Dan. He should be here with me in Mexico. He passed away on May 20, 2014, just six months before we were to come here. Because we had a Platonic relationship, Julian coming here and being my partner was never an issue. Just because our relationship was Platonic did not mean we didn't have a great love for one another. Dan was a fun and caring guy.

Prologue

Have you ever been to one of those sideshow, gypsy fortune tellers? Many would say 'no' because they believe that kind of stuff is poppycock and foolishness. Well, let me tell you. I had a similar thinking until I met a lady named Lori. She happened to be a friend of a friend and during just general conversation, it happened to come up that she did readings. I must admit, some of the things she told me were very interesting. But I was still somewhat skeptical.

It wasn't until several years later, I heard about a lady from England whose name is Betty Foster. She was in the States for a convention and would only be in Atlanta for a few days. A friend told me about her and said it might be interesting to go see her. Still waffling back and forth in my head about the subject, I decided to go and have her do a reading for me.

In the middle of the card table where we sat, there was a tape recorder. She told me the session was going to be recorded. That way, I could refer back to it in times to come. I thought that was really cool. It also showed me she had confidence in what she was going to tell me.

She began explaining what she was doing and gave a sketchy outline as to how the reading would progress. At the beginning, she got into past life experiences. The first one she said that was of import was during the Roman time period and I was a Roman soldier. What was very interesting is she told me there was a taller and darker Roman soldier, standing behind me. I can't explain it but somehow, immediately, I had a sense the soldier was my partner, Phillip, in my present life. It was almost freaky the sensation that came over me when she mentioned it. The story she told about our relationship in that Roman time made sense and I could even equate it to my life with him in the current time period.

What was very interesting is that Phillip didn't even balk when I told him about it. I truly expected him to make negative comments about it but he didn't. I always wondered if he felt as I did that such a thing was possible and we had been together in a past life. It's something we never really discussed.

She continued further with other information until she began speaking of the dead. Again, I was halfhearted about what was happening. "There's someone coming through from the other side. It's your mother. No. It's a mother link. It's your grandmother." Her conversation was about information supposedly from my grandmother but then, she asked me a question. "Is your grandmother's name Mary or Margaret?"

I responded quietly. "No."

"Well. I don't understand." She shook her head. "I see her very clearly. And she's mouthing the letter 'M'."

I was completely shocked. I didn't know this woman from Adam. We had never met before in our lives. She didn't even know I was having a reading until I showed up. And yet, I heard what she'd just said and was astounded. Why? My grandmother's name was Emma but everyone called her Em. What can I say?

And don't hand me this stuff that it was a lucky guess. First of all, she had twenty-six letters to choose from but she picked out of all of them the letter 'M'. At least that's what Betty thought. It was not a letter my grandmother was giving Betty. It was her actual name. 'Em'.

The rest of the session was very interesting and quite informative. She did make reference to several others who had passed on as well as things going on in my life at the time. I believe all previous events and research I'd done on the subject were completely sealed by this session. I was no longer a skeptic.

CHAPTER I

I stood there, looking out to sea. Tears streamed down my face, knowing I had to let go. It was almost ridiculous. I was pining for someone I didn't even remember meeting, except in dreams. None of it made any sense. Even Nick was totally confused about it all. And if what Nick had said was actually true, it made it so much more understandable as to our confusion.

He couldn't have been a figment of my imagination since Nick remembered him from his own dreams. But it was obvious to both of us, he didn't belong here. Was it possible somehow, we both suffered from the same figment of the imagination or delusion? But the dreams were so real.

Neither of us could put the whole puzzle together. My heart was breaking. But for what? A phantom who haunted both of our nights?

Nick patted me on the back as we turned and walked back to the house. Maybe in time, we'd be able to have an understanding as to what happened. We were going to have to try and recall every hour since arriving here back in the spring. If both of us put our heads together, maybe just maybe, we'd find the answers. We could only hope.

CHAPTER II

In nineteen seventy, I was ten years old when we went to a traveling fair that had come to town. It came around every year about the same time in the fall. You know those old-fashioned, traveling carnivals with the Ferris wheel and merry-go-round. I was always so fond of the sideshows. There was the bearded lady, the man who could lift five hundred pounds and the amazing magician. But this time around, I saw a side booth I hadn't seen before. The sign said. 'Know your future! Madame Zelda knows all!'

These kinds of things intrigued me. I knew they could be fake and most likely were but they were fun. They were like the Ouija board. You would play it, knowing everyone was pushing it. Never was there some actual supernatural phenomenon. It was all fun and games. My skepticism always made me wonder. If these folks actually knew the future, why weren't they multimillionaires, having invested wisely in the stock market? Oh, well. What could I say?

I remember it so clearly. My friends, Bobby and John, were with me. We all looked at one another, wondering what we should do, having read the sign.

"Okay, guys. What do you think? Should I go in and find out about my future?" Realizing my age, I started to think about the years ahead. My whole life was out in front of me. "Maybe she can tell me how to become the next millionaire."

Bobby shook his head. "Yeah. Sure. Believe it."

"It's only a buck." John pointed out. "I'll even give you the buck if you'll do it. Just one thing. Bobby and I get to sit in and listen." Like the Cheshire Cat, he gave a huge grin. "We want to find out if you're going to end up marrying Connie Lee."

That made us all break into raucous laughter.

"Okay. Let's go." I paused for a moment. "Wouldn't it be funny as shit if she did say I was going to marry Connie Lee?"

That made us all laugh even harder as we walked to the entrance of the tent.

There was a man, sitting at a table and dressed in clothing people would associate with gypsies. He looked up at us and smiled. "And what can Madame Zelda do for you young gentlemen today? She knows all and sees all."

I handed him the dollar John had given me and smiled. "I wanted to see what Madame Zelda could tell me about my future."

He looked at me with a huge grin. "Well, my boy. You have a whole life ahead of you. She just might be able to tell you what roads to take. I'll see if she is ready to see you." He got up to go into the tent.

I called out. "Will it be all right if my friends sit in on the session? I don't mind."

"If you wish. I don't see it as a problem. One moment. Let me see if she is ready." He went inside the tent.

Within a few minutes, he came out and instructed. "Right this way, gentlemen. Madame Zelda can see you now." He leaned and gestured with his hands in the direction of the entrance to the tent. "Follow the hall."

We walked down a narrow corridor to where the heavy canvas curtain to our left ended. We turned to the left, continuing to follow the corridor that now paralleled the one we had just walked. The heavy canvas curtain was to our left. We continue to walk until we came to an opening on the right. This opening was to a darkened room, looking like some scene out of an old movie.

Sitting behind a table, covered with a thick, embroidered tablecloth, sat a lady dressed just as you would imagine a gypsy fortune teller to be dressed. Immediately, an image of Maria Ouspenskaya from the old Lon Chaney, werewolf movies popped into my head. In front of her, on the table, was a very large, clear glass globe, resting in a brass holder that looked like the spread toes of several chickens' feet.

She looked up at me, smiled then spoke very softly. "Come in, young man. Please, sit down. Let me see what the future has in store for you. Your friends may sit right over there." She gestured with her right hand.

We all sat down in our appropriate places and everything was quiet for a moment.

Still smiling, she looked at me. "Let me see your hands. Palms up."

I stretched out both my arms in front of me, placing them on the table with my palms up, one on either side of the glass globe. This was so exciting to me. I knew it most likely was all a show but it was fun. I wanted to play this to the hilt.

Using the index finger of her right hand, she gently went over the lines in the palms of both my hands. A questioning expression came to her face. She shook her head. Leaning back in her chair, she looked directly at me. "This is very interesting. Very interesting." Then, she placed her hands on either side of the glass globe in front of her and she stared intently into the globe.

I loved it. I felt like I was in a scene from the werewolf movies. I almost expected Lon Chaney to barge in at any moment, looking like the ferocious werewolf.

After a few moments, she began speaking very quietly. "You are going to have a very interesting life. The road you have planned in your mind will not be the road you actually take. Right now, you are young. As you grow older, many things will come to pass. These are things that will be out of the ordinary."

She paused, shaking her head and squinting her face. "I see you in your late thirties. By then, your life will have taken many turns." She paused for a moment. Then, bent forward, looking into the globe again. "The sea. I see the ocean. The ocean is going to have some great significance to you. I am getting strong vibrations regarding that." She sat back in the chair. "You are going to be successful, doing many things. It seems everything is leading you to the ocean in your late thirties. This seems to be extremely important. Remember that. Yes. The ocean is very important."

She paused slightly again. "As you grow older, you may hear from others you are wrong, regarding something very personal but do not believe them. As strange as it may be, you are who you are supposed to be and you will be doing exactly what you are supposed to be doing."

She paused again then looked at me with a questioning expression. "I know this is going to sound very strange and I do not want you to be alarmed. But something is going to happen in your late thirties that will change everything. What is even more unbelievable to me is I cannot see beyond that time period. It has nothing to do with death but it is somehow a new beginning. Even I am not sure what it means." At that, her whole body seemed to relax as she leaned back in the chair again.

We all seemed to sit quietly for a time. Then, I looked at her and very quietly spoke. "I'm not going to marry Connie Lee, am I?" I could hear low snickering from the guys sitting behind me.

She smiled at me and tilted her head to the side. "No, my boy. You're not going to marry Connie Lee. Your road is in another direction." A huge smile filled her face. "That is all I have for you today."

I stood up, bowed my head slightly and smiled back at her. "Thank you. Thank you very much, Madame Zelda."

Sticking out my right hand as if to shake hers, she took my hand in both of hers and smiled back with an extremely sincere look on her face. "Do not worry about what people say. Follow your heart. Follow what YOU think is right. And remember what I said about the ocean." Then, she let my hand go.

I bowed and thanked her again as we turned and left.

When we got outside the tent, Bobby clapped his hands. "Well, I'm glad you're not going to marry Connie Lee. I've always thought she's a stuck-up bitch."

Twenty-nine years have virtually passed since then. Of course, being around ten at the time, none of what the gypsy lady said made a lot of sense to me except I wouldn't marry Connie Lee. I was glad of it but not really understanding why.

CHAPTER III

When I was fourteen, I began to understand why I wasn't going to marry Connie Lee. My interests weren't in that direction. Bobby and John started talking about girls and possible girlfriends. My time was spent differently. I enjoyed painting and playing with my electric trains. Girls and girlfriends were the farthest things from my mind.

As for the ocean being important, I had no clue. Yes. I loved the ocean and the beach. I didn't know many who didn't. Maybe it was a warning of some sort. It didn't make sense since I lived nowhere near the ocean.

It was fall again and the fair was back in town. Bobby, John and I hadn't been since we were ten. I thought what fun it would be to go. After discussing it with Bobby and John, I discovered they were going with their girlfriends. I would have been the odd man. But that didn't deter me. I'd go by myself.

After a ride on the Ferris wheel, the tilt-a-whirl and the bumper cars, I began strolling through the arcades and sideshows. Suddenly, there was a tent in front of me and a sign by the entry. 'Know your future! Madame Zelda knows all!'

I was surprised. Could it be the same one? If so, it would be interesting to see if my future would be different. I walked up to the table at the entry. I wasn't sure but it looked like the same older man who was there before. I also noticed it was no longer a dollar.

It was now five dollars. Inflation. I grinned and handed the man a five-dollar bill I had saved from my allowances and pay for doing odd jobs in the neighborhood like mowing lawns.

He looked at me and smiled. "One moment. Let me see if Madame Zelda is ready." He got up and went into the tent, returning shortly. "She will see you now." His left arm stretched out in the direction of the entrance to the tent.

Yep! Walking through, I finally came to the entrance of the room. Taking a quick look around, I could see nothing had changed. I felt as if I had stepped back four years in time. Everything seemed to be exactly as it was four years earlier. Even Madame Zelda, sitting behind the table. I looked directly at her and smiled.

She looked at me, smiled then a very questioning expression came to her face. She continued looking at me as she spoke. "Come. Please, sit down." She directed with her right hand.

I sat down at the table in front of her, looked back at her and smiled.

After a few moments of silence, she spoke very softly. "I can feel it. You have come to me before. I see your friends are not with you today. Could it be because they are with their girlfriends?" She smiled at me. "But you aren't interested in girlfriends. As I told you before, your life was going to be different. And the ocean. I told you the ocean was important. It still is. Some of what I told you before, you may now possibly understand. You're not like the others. Your path is different. Your interests are different. Do not worry about who you are. It was meant to be this way."

She placed her hands on either side of the glass globe in front of her. As before, she stared deeply into it. Moments later, she placed her hands on the table and leaned back in her chair. "Do not worry that your friends have interests you don't share. It's not important. Your road is going to be extremely different from theirs. As is your life."

Suddenly, her body shook and she looked very hard at me. "Yes. I remember. I remember I couldn't see. Beyond your late thirties.

It's the same even now. For some reason, I cannot see your future beyond your late thirties. But I tell you now as I did before. It has nothing to do with death. It's a new beginning. I do not understand what it is or what it means. But that is all I can tell you. And the ocean. The ocean is very important."

Soon, she smiled. "You are learning. Be yourself and do not worry what others may think or say. You are on your own path, not theirs."

I smiled back at her. "Thank you, Madame Zelda. Thank you very much. I understand much of what you have told me and it has helped me, not to let it bother me." I bowed my head slightly. "Thank you, again, and goodbye." I stood up.

She stood as well. "Goodbye, my child. But. It may not be goodbye. Remember, I am out here should the need ever arise for you to come to me again. Take care of yourself. Continue on your road. It IS the right one."

I was smiling as I left the tent. There was a sense of contentment inside me. I was glad I saw her and talked.

Needless to say, the rest of high school was interesting. Both Bobby and John became big jocks. Bobby joined the wrestling team. John became captain of the football team. I, on the other hand, was president of the art club and very involved in the drama class.

The Senior Prom was another thing. Bobby took his high school sweetheart who he would eventually marry. John took the girl he was dating at the time. As for me, I had no intention of going but Bobby said his sister would love to go with me. What could I say? That decision was easy and allowed me to go with no major problems or obligations.

After graduation, Bobby went to work, eventually taking over his father's service station. John decided to join the service. I heard he became a Navy Seal. I went away to study art and architecture in college. This was a turning point in my life.

CHAPTER IV

In my college Freshman year, I'd shown so much potential with oil painting in my art classes, my teachers had me take more advanced classes along with my architectural classes.

It was the beginning of my Sophomore year in nineteen seventy-nine. I was nineteen. My roommate's name was Nick who was a very good-looking guy, a head taller than myself and at least fifty more pounds. We became immediate, fantastic friends. I have to admit, sometimes I thought about him as more than a friend. I think I'd have liked for certain things to happen but maybe it was best it never did. It was a time we were young but still not fully developed in our emotional thinking.

It was early December right after Thanksgiving when Nick mentioned he'd heard a traveling carnival was coming to town. "How would you like to go? I think it would be a blast. I know you have to be careful. And all those stupid rides, since they put them up overnight. But seriously. It could be a lot of fun."

I agreed. "Oh, hell. Why not? You're right. It could be a lot of fun."

It was a few days later when the carnival arrived and was finally open for business. After classes that Friday, we decided to go. Strolling through the carnival for some reason, it all seemed so familiar to me. I shook my head and snickered.

Nick looked at me. "What's so funny?"

"It's this carnival. It's like I've been here before. It all seems so familiar. I went to one back home in the fall. When I was in early high school. And I would swear I was there again."

"Well. You never know. These things travel around the country. It's the only way they can make any money. They'd never do it, staying in the same place all the time." Nick smiled.

I kept looking around. "Yeah. But what are the chances this would be the same one? The same one I went to when I was ten. That was nine years ago. Just like the one I went to when I was fourteen. And that was five years ago."

Nick clapped his hands. "Hey. True. Nine years is practically half of our life. But for most people who are forty or more, nine years is a walk in the park."

His comment made me understand. "Nick, you do have a point there. But seriously, I'd swear this was the same carnival."

As we walked around, we saw many of the rides. None of them seemed to appeal to us. It was like the old expression. 'Been there! Done that!' We stopped at one of the concession stands and we each bought some cola and a hot dog. It seemed appropriate. We sat down at a nearby table and chairs to eat. I was actually surprised at how tasty the hot dog was.

Continuing through the arcades and sideshows, Nick would make pertinent comments, regarding each one. Like the sideshow with the bearded lady. He would say. "I just know the beard is fake! Yeah. I know it is."

Turning the corner, suddenly, in front of us, was a tent. I stopped short and almost froze, staring at the tent.

Nick gave me a strange look. "What's wrong?"

I spoke softly. "I was right. It IS the same carnival. You see that tent right there?" I pointed. "Look at the sign and tell me what it says."

Nick looked at the sign by the entryway to the tent and he read out loud what was written on it. "Know your future! Madame Zelda knows all!" He turned and looked at me. "So?"

I turned to Nick. "I went to Madame Zelda when I was ten and strangely enough when I was fourteen. Now, here she is again at nineteen."

Nick clapped his hands together. "Wow! I think this is so cool. You have to go. It's like it was meant to be. You can't let this go by. I think this is truly bizarre. And what are the chances?"

"Well, I don't know." I knew myself too well but was afraid something might come out in the session I didn't want Nick to know.

"Oh. Come on. It'll be fun." Nick smiled and jumped up and down.

"Okay. Okay. Let's go." I headed in the direction of the tent with Nick by my side.

There, again, was the older man, sitting at the table. The sign on the table indicated it was now ten dollars.

I questioned. "Would it be all right for my friend to sit in and listen?"

The old man nodded and smiled. "That will be just fine." Just as before, after paying, he left the table to see if Madame Zelda was ready. And just as before, he emerged from the tent with a big smile. "Madame Zelda will see you now."

Nick and I were finally standing at the entry to the room. It was like a déjà vu of stepping back in time. Not one thing had changed. Even Madame Zelda, sitting there. I had to stop from pinching myself to make sure it was real.

Madame Zelda looked up at us without a word. With her right hand, she directed me to sit in the chair in front of her. With her left, she directed Nick to sit in the back.

She sat quietly for a few moments. Suddenly, a very questioning expression came to her face. It was one of searching through umpteen memories. Then, she spoke very quietly. "I know you." She tilted her head, scrutinizing Nick, sitting behind me. She got a rather sly look on her face and stared at me. "I see you have come to understand one of the things I told you before. You are finding yourself but you're not finished yet." She slowly shook her head in the affirmative. "Yes. It will be the sea. The sea will bring you to fruition. I feel your friend here is not like you but you are very good friends. That is a good thing. Close and reliable friends are a valued gift. This man will be an excellent friend for the rest of time. Never hesitate to confide in him. He senses and knows who you are and it's of no consequence to him. It is the friendship you share with him that is most important."

She tilted her head forward and gazed into the glass ball in front of her. "I see a time the man who is here with you today will be someone you will rely on in the future."

I looked right at her and smiled. "Madame Zelda, I must tell you. To me, it's amazing. It is you I have happened upon when coming to the carnival. Not once. Not twice. But now, for a third time, over a nine-year period. To be honest with you, there has always been some skepticism on my part. But now, having come to you for the third time and you recognizing and knowing me as you have, totally astounds me. The information you have given me every time has opened a door to my understanding of who I am and the road I am taking. I'm extremely grateful to you. Without the information you have given me, all the times I had questioned myself, I heard your voice and your knowledge coming through. I realize now, these were intersections in the road where I needed to make a decision as to which one to take. What you told me in the past helped me choose the ones I did."

I looked down at the glass globe on the table and shook my head. "I mean. What are the chances that every single time I came to a carnival, you are the lady who would be here for me to seek my fortune? This may sound very weird but I truly believe the Fates have led me to you every time."

My hands happen to be resting on the table. She grabbed my right one with both hands and smiled at me. "My child, you are correct. The Fates work in mysterious ways. Every time I have seen you come through my door, it made me know they had brought you to me. It was not coincidence. I also know if there comes a time you need me again, the Fates will lead you to me."

She smiled and released my hand. "Now, go. Find your Destiny with the sea. I still cannot explain or understand it. But I wasn't meant to. I was just the instrument to help you understand your Destiny is there. Why I cannot see beyond that point eludes me but I'm sure it's for a reason. I do know this. I feel it. You will find happiness there. Great happiness. So. Follow your road. Follow your heart. Take your time. You will get there when you're supposed to get there. Not to worry. In the meantime, go live your life and be happy. As I told you before, Madame Zelda is out here. If you ever need me again, the Fates will lead you to me again." A warmth came over her face as she smiled.

I stood up and reached for my wallet. "Madame Zelda. Please, don't be offended as that is not my intent. It is the only way right now, I have to express my appreciation to you." I went into my wallet and found a twenty-dollar bill. I turned to Nick.

Nick realized without words being spoken. He stood up, went to his wallet and opened it in my direction.

I looked in and saw a twenty-dollar bill. I took it out and looked at Nick. "I promise. I WILL pay you back."

Placing my wallet back in my pocket, I then turned and took the two twenty-dollar bills and placed them on the table next to the glass globe. I looked at Madame Zelda and smiled. "Please, take this as a token of my appreciation. I thank you very much."

She stood up with a huge smile and walked around the table with her arms outstretched. Within moments, she was giving me a big hug. I returned it and hugged her tightly. She whispered to me. "I know it will all be good. You are a kind and considerate man. Do not worry. You will find your happiness with the sea. Now go, my child, and know Madame Zelda wishes you all the best." She turned to Nick who had stood. She walked over to him. "Your Destiny is connected to his. Remember that. Watch over your friend and take care of him. Keep him on the right path. You both were meant to be friends forever in this life." She hugged him tightly, pulled away, looked up into his face and gave him a big smile.

Nick smiled. "I will. I definitely will. Thank you."

We both bowed slightly and smiled before we turned to go.

Nick and I slowly walked outside the tent and bowed slightly to the older man, sitting at the table as we walked by. Walking slowly, neither of us spoke for a while.

Suddenly, I stopped, turned and looked at Nick. "You know? She said you knew. Why didn't you tell me?"

Nick smiled and shook his head. "If it's what I think it is, it's of no consequence. You are you. I like you for you. It doesn't matter you don't like the same things I do." He shook his head. "And if you think there is a problem because we're roommates, just sweep that right out of your mind. I have no problem with it and us being roommates."

I looked at Nick and smiled. "Thank you for that. It is something I've been dealing with for a long time but have never acted on it. Oh. Not to say there haven't been those times."

"I'm sure it's just like me. Seeing some of these hot coeds on campus but never acting on it."

A surprised expression came to my face. "But Nick, you're one good-looking man. I'm sure any girl would like to go out with you."

"But I don't have time to get all tied up in that kind of shit. My education is way more important than having a little fling now and then. I don't want to get stuck, if you know what I mean, with some albatross around my neck when I'm not ready for it."

I nodded. "You've got that right."

As we walked along, Nick spoke quietly. "And she was right. If you ever want to talk, let's do it. Talk, that is." He flexed his eyebrows and grinned. "And remember, she told you we were friends forever. She was absolutely correct. I believe we WILL be friends for life. Know I will always be here for you."

CHAPTER V

After graduation, Nick and I continued to stay in close touch. We never got to visit one another but occasionally would send photos. I swear I believe he got more handsome as time progressed. As handsome as he was, the original physical attraction in the very beginning changed and went away. He was now like a brother to me.

He was correct about his education. He became a very successful engineer and married about two years after graduation.

I didn't do badly as an architect. I was hired by an Atlanta architectural firm and before I knew it, I had moved way up on the ladder in the company. Many of the firm's clients were requesting me to be their architect as they'd seen some of my work and were extremely impressed with it. Needless to say, money was finally no object in my life.

My oil paintings were in a few galleries in the Atlanta area. One in particular that I liked was Roger's Gallery located in Midtown. The owner was a terrific guy with a great sense of humor. Even one major gallery in New York was showing and selling my paintings. I was very pleased.

It was about ten years after graduation, nineteen ninety-two and I was thirty-two. I got a call from Nick. He was going through a divorce. I told him how sorry I was but he told me not to worry. The more he thought about it the more he wondered why they married in the first place. He was just glad there were no children.

"And by the way, I've been transferred. YeeeHaw! Moving up in the company. They're opening a main office in Atlanta and want me to run it. What do you think of that?"

"Well. Let me throw this out. Why don't you come stay with me while you're looking for a place of your own? And I swear, I'll keep my hands to myself."

I began to chuckle and heard Nick chuckling as well.

"You mean to tell me you don't have a significant other yet?" Nick had surprise in his voice.

"No. Just those occasional one-night stands. None of them were meaningful. What can I say?"

"Well, if that's the case, I'd love to take you up on your offer. Just keep me posted as to the monthly expenses, so I can pay my share."

The ten years I'd not seen Nick had been incredibly kind to him. With his dark brown hair, he now sported a nicely trimmed beard and mustache which looked incredible on him. He was more handsome than ever. I had to keep reminding myself that we were friends.

October, about three months after Nick moved in, I was going through a copy of an architectural magazine and happened to see pictures and an article, regarding a home built on the east coast of Mexico, overlooking the Gulf. One thing that really caught my eye was the costs involved. It got me thinking. "Oh, hell! Why not!"

When we both got home from work that night and I was fixing dinner, I had Nick sit down at the table and started telling him about my idea. "Okay. I know you think it's probably insane but why not?"

Nick just gave a big grin and shook his head. "To be honest with you, I think it's a great idea. You're young, you have the money and you're an architect. I'll bet you could design an incredible house down there. And who knows? It could end up in that famous architectural magazine."

I served our plates and sat down. "I know this is going to sound really impromptu but I heard you mention the other day you have two weeks coming to you and if you don't take them, you'll lose them. I have time coming to me as well. Let me do a little research and see what I can find and maybe next month go down for a two-week vacation."

Nick had already started eating. "Actually, I don't think it's insane. I think it's an absolutely incredible idea. You'll have a vacation home to go to and when you're not there, you can rent it. Then, when you're ready to retire, you'll have a great place that's just waiting for you." He paused for a moment, looked up and grinned. "And by the way, you are such an amazing cook. One of these days you're going to make someone a great wife."

I looked at Nick and we both began to roar with laughter.

That night before going to bed, I went online and started searching for properties in Mexico. Strangely enough, I found this real estate agent who lived in Zihuatanejo on the southwest coast. Why the west coast? There are virtually no hurricanes. The east coast is constantly being hit with hurricanes in the Gulf. The one thing I did have to contend with would be an occasional tremor. After all, that area is on the 'Ring of Fire'. I emailed her, asking about property there. As I went to bed, I couldn't wipe the big smile off my face, thinking about the decision I'd made.

It was two days later I received several emails from the real estate agent. Attached to the emails were a number of pictures. The lot she indicated was amazing. It was right on the beach. With the views looking up and down the beach, I could see the area was very secluded. This meant it would be quiet and serene. I loved it. One of the pictures showed the ocean with many volcanic rocks, projecting from the ocean as well as the beach. I could only imagine the sound of the surf, crashing on them. How could I possibly resist?

I immediately emailed her, requesting information on the lot and if I could see it and do the paperwork in the coming month. A return email from her indicated there would be no problem. And when she quoted the price for the lot, it was a done deal.

When I told Nick about it, I believe he was more excited about it than I was. "I've already told them at work about the possible two-week leave next month just before Thanksgiving and it's no problem. I think this is fantastic. Let's book our tickets now."

"She did recommend a place for us to stay in Troncones. This is a little town about thirty miles up the coast from Zihuatanejo. She said the lot is about twenty miles farther up the coast. When we got there, she said she would meet us at the hotel in Troncones."

What can I say? We were both excited about the trip and what it meant for the future. I had to admit, the things Madame Zelda had told me were in the back of my mind.

CHAPTER VI

We rented a car at the airport in Zihuatanejo, so we'd have transportation. The weather was considerably warmer than early November in Atlanta. The day after we arrived, we all drove up to the lot. The real estate agent was concerned it might be so secluded I wouldn't be interested. I indicated seclusion was exactly what I was looking for.

Seeing the lot as well as the surrounding area, it was a no-brainer. Nick was also enamored with the lot. Seeing the area and realizing the cost of a lot, Nick started contemplating buying one, too. "Hey! I could buy the lot right next to yours and we could be neighbors." He smiled. "And I already know who my architect would be." He flexed his eyebrows.

While there, she introduced us to a builder, indicating he was very good. She even took us to see some of the homes he had constructed. Being an architect, I was extremely pleased with his work. Seeing how pleased I was, she arranged a meeting, so I could talk with him. Indicating I had house plans virtually ready to go, I would email him scaled copies for his use. Knowing the structure was going to be one-story high, he gave a ballpark figure as to price per square foot. I was incredibly pleased and knew the eighteen hundred square foot design I had would be well within the range of what I planned to spend. What was also pleasing is the house would be finished in six to eight months. That meant we could go down on vacation the next year in July or August.

Nick couldn't stand it. He told the real estate agent he wanted the lot right next to mine. He also told the builder after he finished my house, he could probably begin on his. Nick grinned, looking at me. "Hey! I'm going to have you do the drawings for the house, you're such a great architect. And remember. I told you long ago we would be friends for life."

We both did a 'thumbs-up' then high-fived.

Because we were such good friends and got along exceedingly well, Nick became a permanent roommate at the apartment in Atlanta. He told me that the slight hint of turpentine smell from my painting was not a problem. I told him I would keep the third bedroom door closed to keep it at a minimum.

He just responded. "Hey! Artists need their space and consideration."

We would pal around together because we just enjoyed each other's company. He would periodically go out on a date with some girl he met through one of those dating services then the conversations we'd have at dinner afterward just proved she was 'not the one'. I, also, had my tales to tell of my dates with guys who were 'not the one'.

I also sat down with Nick and began to discuss the kind of house he wanted. Having known him for so many years, I had a basic idea as to what he was looking for. I also had a sense it was going to be a bachelor's house. It's not I wished Nick to remain single, it's just I had a sense he wasn't the marrying kind. He liked his freedom too much. His house would be a definite complement to mine next door.

In September, a little more than two years after Nick moved in, he came home and mentioned one of his big clients was having a birthday party for his wife and wanted both of us to come. "Yes.

I told him I had a roommate who was an incredible architect and he insisted I bring you along. He said he'd like to meet you and get to talk sometime about designing a vacation home on a beach somewhere. It should be a lot of fun because he's hired clowns and jugglers and entertainment like that, so the guests would have a good time. It's this coming weekend. How does that sound to you?"

A big smile filled my face. "Why not. I don't have anything planned for this weekend at all. It should be fun."

We left the house by late morning that Saturday as the party was going to be out in Conyers, east of Atlanta. Arriving at the location, we found a large field where people were parking. With the number of cars there already, there had to be at least two hundred guests at the party. Nick and I parked the car and headed in the direction of the very large house in the distance.

The closer we got to the house, we could hear the revelry and see tents set up all over the place. There was even a live band. It truly was a huge event. It took a while to find our host and his wife, so we could wish her a happy birthday. The main event was not going to be until later on in the late afternoon along with a cookout. Drinks would start around two in the afternoon.

The host smiled then snickered. "I don't care what time it is. Let's get you guys a cocktail." At that, he dragged us to the bar and had the bartender fix us both a Bloody Mary. He put his finger up to his lips and looked around at the other guests. He whispered. "Mum's the word." A big Cheshire Cat grin filled his face. With that kind of attitude, I knew that when I got to talk with him, I was going to really like him. He was going to make a terrific client.

Nick and I grabbed our secret cocktails and sat at one of the tables on the terrace. We thought it best to get our bearings before strolling around the venue. While sitting at the table, one of the clowns came by doing cartwheels and somersaults. I could see another in the distance doing juggling. One guy was going around, doing a fire-eating act. I had to admit the atmosphere was quite festive.

Finally, finishing our drinks, we got up and started walking around. Several of the tents set up had specialty foods. One had a puppet show. Another had a magician.

Then, I saw something I couldn't believe. "Nick! Tell me I'm not seeing what I think I see." I pointed in the direction of a tent set up in the back area.

"Oh, my God! I don't believe it. It can't be the same one." He read out loud the words on the sign in front of the tent. "Know your future! Madame Zelda knows all!" He turned and looked at me. "You don't think it could actually be the same one we went to when we were in college, do you?"

I turned and looked at him. "Well. There's one way to find out." I started walking toward the tent with Nick right there with me.

Sitting at a table by the entrance was an old man, dressed in gypsy clothing, collecting money. He looked up at us with a smile. "Have you come to have Madame Zelda tell your fortune?"

I reached in my back pocket and pulled out my wallet. Opening it, I got out the fifteen dollars to pay my admission. "Would it be all right if my friend accompanies me? He's not going to have his fortune told."

The old man smiled. "That's not a problem. Go right in. Madame Zelda is waiting."

Nick and I followed the well-remembered corridor to the entry of an interior room. We stopped and looked through the entryway. The room was exactly the same. Nothing, not one single thing had changed. And there, sitting behind the table, with a large glass globe in front of her, was Madame Zelda, looking the same as when I first saw her.

She looked up from the glass globe and gazed into my eyes. I watched her face. First, there was a questioning expression. Then, it instantly changed to one of recognition. A huge smile filled her face and she spoke softly. "Come in, my child. It has been a long time. Come, sit down and we will talk." She gestured with her right hand as Nick took a seat in the back.

The last time I saw Madame Zelda, I was nineteen. Now, I was just over thirty-four. Remembering she had told me I'd be finding my Destiny in my late thirties, from my perspective, that wasn't far off. Looking at her, I smiled.

She spoke softly. "You are a handsome young man and very successful in business. I am glad." She leaned over, looking around me, peering at Nick. "I see your good friend is still with you. I am glad of that as well. I feel he has been very successful. Very good. And he is a very handsome man, too. I like his beard and mustache. They look very good on him." She gave a big smile then turned to me. "You are almost there. Your Destiny. The sea is calling you. In time, you will understand." A questioning expression came to her face as she shook her head. "It is very strange. I'm still unable to see beyond. There seems to be some kind of invisible wall, blocking me. There are no vibrations of evil or death but I cannot see any farther. I do feel that beyond that point, you will find your Destiny and happiness. That's all I'm able to understand."

Speaking softly, I looked at her. "I must tell you. About two years ago, I obtained property by the ocean. It is beautiful there. Quiet and secluded. Perfect for relaxation. The house was finished last year and we went down and spent our vacation there. You won't believe it but my friend, Nick, here, is building a house there right next door to me."

She looked at Nick and then at me. "I'm so glad. I'm glad he will be close to you. You seem to be happy. You have taken the correct roads to reach your Destiny. You're almost there. You may not realize it when it's happening but go with your heart. That's all that matters. Your friend's Destiny is connected to yours. I do not know quite how it will all go but you both will be friends forever."

She looked at me very hard and smiled. "My child, I believe I won't see you again until we are in the great beyond. Know I wish you joy and happiness for the rest of your life and may all good things come to you. The Fates have brought us together these many times. I now know that. I believe it was to make sure you were taking the right road. I say goodbye to you, my child. Now, go and have a good life and find that Destiny in the sea. Go with your heart." Her eyes glinted and a huge smile filled her face.

We all stood up together. She came around the table with open arms. We hugged each other tightly. Then, she pulled back and looked at Nick. "Come." Nick walked over beside me and was silent. Madame Zelda opened her arms and hugged him tightly. "As I told you before, take care of your friend and keep him on the right path. But there will come a time you must let him go. You will have to let him go. I think you will understand." She paused for a moment. "But. It may not be over quite yet when that happens. Somehow, I still feel you both will continue to be good friends for life." She took her left arm and wrapped it around Nick and her right arm around me, pulling us to her as if we were her sons. After a few moments, she let us go and stood back.

I looked directly at her. "Madame Zelda, thank you. Thank you very much. Know I will remember you for the rest of my days. You will forever remain in my thoughts and my heart. Please, take this as a token of my appreciation." I reached in my back pocket and pulled out my wallet. I turned to Nick, who began doing the same. In my wallet were three fifty-dollar bills. I pulled them out. Nick extended his wallet in my direction. Interestingly enough, he also had three fifty-dollar bills in his wallet. I took the six bills and laid them on the table next to the glass globe. "Goodbye, Madame Zelda. I thank you forever for your wisdom and advice."

She looked at me very hard and smiled. "Thank you both for your generosity and kindness." She looked at Nick. "Take care of your friend." She smiled at both of us. "Go, my children, and be happy."

I smiled as we turned and left. I knew I would never see her again in this life.

As we slowly walked from the tent, Nick spoke very quietly. "Damn. What just happened? I feel like I have just left a greatly loved auntie. Geez. I think I need a drink."

"Nick. Not to worry about your money. You know I'm good for it. It was important."

"Yeah. I got that. And don't sweat the money. It will never be able to touch the fun we're having in Mexico on our vacations. We should be able to head down in two months, right after Thanksgiving. The builder said my house should be finished by then. I can't wait to actually walk through it."

We returned to the main house, stopping along the way for a couple of munchies. Then, we went to the main bar and ordered another cocktail. Sitting there for over an hour and talking about what had happened, we decided to walk around to look and see some of the festivities and what was in some of the other tents.

We both slowly strolled around for a while until we came to the area where Madame Zelda's tent was located. We looked at one another and were totally shocked when we reached the area where it was before and it was no longer there. We turned around, perusing the area and could not imagine what had happened to it.

Nick scratched his head. "I know it was right here. Where did it go?" He slowly turned around in a circle again to make sure he was in the right place. "This is weird as shit."

I stood there, shaking my head. I knew we were in the right place. "Nick. It's gone. You are absolutely correct. This IS weird as shit. I never heard or saw it leave. I don't know what to say."

Nick reached up and scratched his head. "Now, I really do need another drink." He started making the sounds of the opening notes to the old TV show, 'The Twilight Zone'. "De de de de. De de de de."

We began walking back. But realized we had taken another route. It didn't matter. We just might see some other interesting concessions. We kept walking.

Suddenly, Nick stopped. "Look!" He pointed at a tent. It looked like Madame Zelda's but there was no sign. We ran over to it.

There was an older man, sitting at the entrance but he was different. He looked at us and smiled. "Would you like your fortunes told?"

Nick smiled and looked at me. "Something's not right here. I'm going to check this out and see if she's inside." He looked at the old man and smiled. "Yes. I would like to have mine told." He handed the man the fifteen-dollar fee. "Would it be all right if my friend comes with me?"

There was a scowl expression on his face. "We usually don't do that without a charge." He shook his head.

I looked at Nick. "You're right. Something's not right. I'll wait here for you. Not a problem. Go in." I ushered with both hands.

Nick entered the tent. In about four minutes, he came slowly walking out of the tent. He was looking at the ground, shaking his head and speaking softly. "It's not her. It's not her. It's not Madame Zelda. Where did she go?" He looked at me and a crazy look filled his face. "Something very weird and strange has happened here today. Yep. Something really strange. Now, I REALLY DO need a drink."

We headed back to the bar. Both of us realized something totally out of the ordinary and unexplainable had happened. It would be the focal point of many future conversations.

The party at the home of Nick's client was just over four years ago. Through the years, we found ourselves spending our vacations together. Where? Of course! At the houses in Mexico. Nick even started surfing. The town of Saladita was some twenty miles down the coast from the house and seemed to be a place that was very nice for surfing.

I finally had time to paint and practice piano. I had the older one shipped down after purchasing another. I did have to have the strings replaced with plated ones to keep them from rusting in the salty air. Life was good for both of us.

CHAPTER VII

It was the spring of nineteen ninety-eight. Vacation time came early this year. Originally, we were going to come later in the year in mid-June. It was to celebrate our birthdays. We were going to be thirty-eight. But that had to be changed because Nick had a big project, going to begin in early summer. Nick promised we'd definitely go the next year, nineteen ninety-nine, in June. But we were really gearing up for the celebrating of our fortieth birthday in the year two thousand. It would not only be the beginning of a new decade for us, a new century and also the beginning of a new millennium. We'd both make sure nothing would stand in the way of that vacation.

We were just about ready to come down for the first two weeks in May when an emergency situation at work made it impossible for Nick to go. He was not a happy camper. "But you know the old expression. 'Business before pleasure.' What can I say? If I can get it fixed in time, I'll come down and join you. Would hate to see you all alone down there in the middle of spring in all that wonderful paradise. But if I get started on this project now, I should be able to get it done by May sixth. I think that's a Wednesday. That would mean I can come down on that Thursday."

It was late morning when I arrived at the airport in Zihuatanejo. Saturday, the second of May. Before getting to the house, I stopped and bought groceries to last a couple of days. Totally exhausted, I decided to take a nap. By the time I woke up, the sun was going down, so I went out onto the terrace. As usual, the sunset was very beautiful.

It was strange not having Nick there. I actually missed him. He'd been working very hard the week before I left to get his project finished as soon as possible. He was supposed to meet his clients on Monday and Tuesday to discuss the project. If all went well, he would be finished by Wednesday. I hoped for his sake, it would go smoothly. It would mean he could come down on Thursday, May the seventh as he'd wanted.

As the light of day began to fade, I decided to take a walk on the beach. The lights were off in the house as electricity here isn't cheap. I tried to conserve it as much as possible. One reason I was planning on installing solar panels on the roof.

Grabbing a glass of my freshly made Margarita batch, I headed out the door. There was no hurry. I was just enjoying the peace and serenity. Night began to take over the sky. It was filled with a million stars, just one of the huge advantages of not being in the city.

Finally, my eyes became accustomed to the darkness. Periodically, I would turn and look out to sea, watching the waves crash on the rocks, jutting from the surface.

I'd walked about thirty minutes up the beach, turned and was just about home again when I stopped to look out at the ocean. That's when I noticed a very small, single light appear far out in the water just beyond the rock formations. I thought it had to be someone doing a little night fishing. I stood there and watched. The light would move to the right and then to the left, going back and forth several times. That's when I realized, it was getting closer to shore.

Continuing to watch it, I saw it come through a group of rocks, through the surf and to the beach almost directly in front of the house. Whatever it was or whoever it was, it was now between me and the house.

My curiosity got the best of me and I began walking in the direction of the light. Getting closer even in the dark, I could see it was a shirtless man in an inflatable raft with a small light attached to the top of his head. He was so busy, pulling the raft ashore, he didn't notice me walking up.

I must have been about fifteen feet from him when I called out without thinking. "¡Hola!"

The sound of my voice must have startled him because he dropped the raft, stood up quickly and turned in my direction. The light on his head was shining directly at me and into my eyes. He said nothing.

What had I done? What if he's some drug person, bringing drugs ashore? Maybe if I sound friendly. "¡Hola!" I called out again. "¿Cómo estás?" Of course, in the bright light, I could see nothing.

He just stood there, looking in my direction, saying nothing.

"Mi español es no bien." I tried to explain in a friendly manner. "Damn! I know my Spanish is terrible but anyone here should be able to understand that."

That's when he reached up, turned off the light on his head and began to chuckle. He then spoke with a deep resounding voice, similar to that of Sam Elliott's. "Yes. Yes, I did. But something tells me Spanish is not your native language." He looked right at me. "I'm sorry. But you did startle me. There's not supposed to be anyone on this beach, especially at this time of the evening. I had told myself. 'Tristan. You should arrive during the day, so you don't hit the rocks and blow out the raft.' But I didn't get here soon enough. Sorry about the light blinding you."

"Oh, shit! So. Tristan! You're a drug trafficker?! And now, you're going to kill my ass for seeing you come ashore!"

"No. No drugs. Nothing like that. But from the last survey done on this long stretch of beach, there was nothing out here and there was no indication there would be for some time. So. There wasn't supposed to be anyone here, either. Okay. The survey was done quite a few years ago. Sorry."

"Well, why the hell would anybody want to come to a deserted stretch of beach, in the dark, unless you were some damn drug lord or doing something that's not legal?"

"Nothing illegal. It's just I needed to get away. And think about things. This seemed to be the perfect place to do it. A little camping on the beach and doing some fishing. I just happened to arrive in the dark. I am sorry. I had no idea you were here. I guess I could go and find another beach somewhere."

"No! No. Don't be ridiculous. You're here. And it's totally cool. Why don't you come up to the house? If you drink, have a Margarita with me?" I raised my empty glass in the air. "Now. I don't know about you but I haven't eaten all day. It's been a very long day. I'm going to fix some ham sandwiches. That should hold us. We can sit on the terrace. Come on. Let's go to the house. You're not Jewish, are you? I mean, the ham and all."

"I would like that. I'd like that very much. And no, I'm not Jewish." He grabbed one of the handles on the raft. "Would you mind if I drag my raft along? It has all my gear in it."

"Not a problem. Bring it on. Here. Let me help you." I grabbed another handle on the other side of the raft. When I did, it gave me a chance to look down and see his feet. I noticed the front ends were somewhat wider than normal and a little bit extended. They almost had the appearance of flippers you buy in a sporting goods store but not as long. Immediately, I felt a touch of sadness. Maybe it was a birth defect. I might bring it up in conversation later.

He smiled. "Thank you. Thank you very much."

As we headed to the house, even in the darkness, I could see he was an incredibly handsome man. He had to be at least several inches over six feet tall, thick dark hair, beard and mustache, with dark hair on his legs, lower arms and covering his chest and stomach. From his build, I'd have sworn he'd been at the gym every day of his life since he was ten. To say, I was very interested in finding out who Mr. 'Tristan' Neptune was would be a huge understatement.

It's not every day a man like this comes out of the ocean to your very front door.

As we walked along, I asked. "So, Tristan. Where are you from? Do you live around in this area?"

He just snickered a bit. "No. I'm not from here. I'm from far, far away." He said nothing more.

Of course, this piqued my curiosity but I didn't want to push it. I'm sure he had his reason for not explaining further. I'd address it another time.

We pulled the raft up onto the terrace, being careful not to damage or poke holes in it.

"Have a seat out here and I'll go get us those Margaritas. Back in a second." I turned on the terrace lights then went into the house to get our drinks.

Tristan looked down at the swim trunks he had on and called out. "I'm still wet. Are you sure it's all right for me to sit down?"

I yelled back. "Hey. This place is for fun and comfort, not formality. Have a seat. I call this place 'La Casa Sans Souci'."

Tristan called out. "Very interesting, mixing Spanish and French. 'The House Without Worry.' I like it."

Refilling my glass, I poured him one. When handing him his drink, I noticed his hand. Between his fingers was skin similar to that between the toes of a duck. Again, I felt sad. Such a handsome man with these birth defects. I said nothing about it. "I'll be right back with the sandwiches. Just give me a few." I headed back to the kitchen, made the sandwiches and placed them on plates.

Finally, returning to the table, I placed one sandwich on the table in front of him and the other where I was sitting and sat down. I'd made his sandwich a lot bigger than mine since he was a much bigger man than me. "Yes. This should hold us for a while."

He smiled. "Thank you. Thank you very much."

When we finished eating, I commented. "I must tell you. I hope you don't mind. Before we get into any major conversation, it's been a very long day for me and I'm exhausted. I've traveled a long way to get here. I have no idea how long you have been out there in the water but what do you think of hitting the hay and getting up tomorrow morning with a fresh start. Forget about your plan of tenting on the beach. There's no way you're going to go out there and sleep. I'll fix breakfast in the morning and we can sit out here on the terrace. We can talk all day long if you like. How does that sound?"

"Actually, that sounds very good. I, too, have been traveling all day and come a very, very long way. A good rest would do me good. Thank you. But I don't want to be any imposition."

"Don't be ridiculous. If I had minded, I'd never have offered the invite. There's three bedrooms in the house and all of them are ready."

We got up, placed the dishes in the sink and headed to the bedrooms. I opened the door to the guest room closest to the main bathroom in the hall.

"This is wonderful. Thank you." He smiled.

"The bathroom is right down the hall here. Everything is in there to take a shower and brush your teeth. Toothbrushes are in the cabinet." I turned to leave the room. "Sleep as late as you like in the morning. There's no time schedule here."

"Thank you again and I'll see you in the morning." He bowed his head slightly.

I headed to my room, took a quick shower in the master bath and was finally in bed. My mind was going crazy as to who Mr. Neptune might be. I whispered in the dark. "Tristan. Nice name. Sounds kinda Norse?" I started to giggle. "Wonder if I should ask him where is Isolde?" What can I say? I couldn't help myself.

Finally, lying there for a few moments, it became evident how tired I really was. Before I knew it, I was asleep.

CHAPTER VIII

Waking up, I felt significantly better. Traveling, regardless of how comfortable, totally wears me out. Stretching out my arms, I felt like a new person.

Immediately, I remembered the stranger from the sea. Did I dream it? Was he a figment of my imagination? Was it an actual event? Was it my mind playing tricks on me from being so tired? An amazingly handsome man like that just doesn't appear out of thin air or in this case the ocean. Yes. It had to have been my mind, playing tricks on me. But what if he isn't a figment? And how is it possible I fell asleep so quickly? I knew nothing about this man. He could be an axe murderer. This thought made me snicker. "I've never seen an axe murderer who looked like that. Not that he couldn't be one. Guess my mind thought he was all right."

I got out of bed, put on a T-shirt and shorts and headed out to cook breakfast. As I left the bedroom, I heard the door to the guest room open.

There he stood in his bathing suit. I couldn't believe how handsome a man he was. The crazy person inside my head was jumping up and down and screaming out. "He's real! He's real! He really is here. YeeeHaw!" I immediately had to calm myself before the crazy person in my head got out.

He looked at me and smiled. "Good morning."

Smiling back, I answered. "Good morning to you. Let's go have some breakfast. Go sit out on the terrace and I'll be out shortly. How about a cup of coffee? I have some nice hazelnut creamer to go in it."

"That sounds good. Thank you." He headed out and sat at the table on the terrace. "I have a pair of shorts in my canvas bag. Thought I'd get those as my swim trunks are still a little damp. I hung them on the hook on the door in the bedroom last night, so I didn't get the bed wet."

"Why don't you take your things and put them in your bedroom, so you don't have to keep coming out here to get stuff."

"Thanks. I do appreciate that."

"Just hang your swim trunks in the bathroom. There's a hook in the shower."

He grabbed his duffel bag and took it to his room. After a few minutes, he returned, wearing his shorts and T-shirt and sat down.

As we ate our omelets and drank our coffee, I noticed his raft. In it were a couple of metal polls and a folded item made of canvas. It was his tent and the metal supports for it. In one corner, there was also a small anchor with a fairly large amount of small rope attached to it. In the other corner, was a speargun. I knew it would be great for underwater fishing. There was also what looked like a tackle box that most likely contained his fishing-related items.

Before I could even question the items, he spoke. "I was going to pitch a tent on the beach and chill out for about a week. Planned to catch a few things out of the ocean to eat." He looked at me and smiled. "Guess I don't have to worry about that anymore. Thank you, so very much."

"You're more than welcome. I know you're going to use your raft again, so why don't you take out the tent and poles and put them over on the terrace since you don't need them right now. Put your tackle box there, too."

He smiled. "That would be great." He got up, grabbed said items and placed them against the outside wall of the house under the roof of the terrace. Then, he came and sat down again.

I continued. "I hope the bed was comfortable."

A big grin filled his face. "It was excellent. I slept like a log."

"Okay. I guess the Inquisition begins. I'll be Torquemada. First question. Why in blue blazes would you come to some deserted shore to kick back and contemplate things in your head?" I was looking right at him.

That's when I first could actually see his amazingly beautiful, blue eyes. They looked like smooth pieces of blue ice. And as he looked at me, I got a sensation he could see into my soul. His eyes were so intense, it was almost unsettling.

He looked at me, smiling and shook his head. Then, he sat straight up in his chair, slowly turned his head in all directions, peering to the horizon. After a moment, he looked back at me. "Why in blue blazes would YOU come to some deserted shore, not only to kick back and contemplate things in your head but to build a house as well?" He continued to smile. His point was made.

"Touché!" I started clapping my hands and shaking my head. "Touché! All right. You got me on that one."

We both started to laugh.

He shook his head with a smile. "Well?"

"Hey! I'm the head inquisitor here. I asked first." I bent my head down, knowing if I kept looking at him I would start laughing again.

He began. "Okay. To be honest with you, I'm not sure where to begin." Looking down, he paused for a few moments. Then, he looked at me and continued. "My parents are bugging me to death about taking over. But it's a huge responsibility and I'm not sure I can handle it. Everyone says I'm ready but I don't know. Mom and Dad want to fade back and enjoy their later years without so much responsibility, hanging over their heads. I understand that. And I must admit. It's past time for me to take over. Also, I just know they're looking for me to get married. They've said nothing, not one thing but I'm so past that age. I swear. Parents can be such a pain in the ass."

I grinned and raised my eyebrows. "Wow. Marriage. That story has a very familiar ring. Unfortunately, I'm not the marrying kind.

At least in the way, everyone thinks about it. Truly. I feel for you. Especially, if there's a big family business involved."

He continued. "It's just I've never found the right..." He paused momentarily. "The right one." He shook his head.

I was in total agreement. "Hey. I sure as hell can identify with that. How about another cup of coffee. And when we finish that, we'll start with some Bloody Marys. Hey! As Jimmy Buffett and Alan Jackson sing it: 'It's five o'clock somewhere.' When I'm on vacation, I get totally relaxed and chill out." I got up and poured more coffee.

With the continuing conversation, along came my boring history of growing up, college years and becoming an architect living in Atlanta.

A questioning expression came to Tristan's face. "I've noticed through your entire story you haven't mentioned anyone special. Seems you haven't found the 'right one', either. Your friend, Nick, seems to be the only one of major import in your life right now."

I smiled. "Well. You're right. As I've said, Nick goes back to my college years. We got along well in school and when he got a divorce, he moved in with me. That was about six years ago. He's sort of been my 'right-hand man' since sophomore year in school. We're like brothers. Probably more than brothers. Kinda like Mutt and Jeff. He knows me like a book. What can I say?" I looked in the direction of Nick's house. "The house next door? That's Nick's house. He always joked we'd be friends for life. To prove it, he bought the lot next door and built a house on it. You'd like Nick. I don't know anyone who doesn't. He's a totally cool, understanding and considerate guy. Now. Your turn."

Strangely, his story was very much like my own. His advanced education seemed to be a lot more diverse than mine was. One thing I found very interesting is he loved antique cars. He indicated he had a garage with several old cars in it. I never pressed the issue as to what they were because I'd have never known their significance or importance.

During his years of education, he was on the swim team. Telling about it made him giggle and shake his head. "Everyone always used to say. 'Oh, hell. Let's see if anyone can beat Tristan this time.' Not to pat myself on the back but I was a very good swimmer. Seems every time I entered a swim meet, I came home with the awards. Mom and Dad were always so proud."

"I think that's so totally cool. But I have one question. Wouldn't all that fur on your body slow you down in the water?" I couldn't help but look directly at his muscular furry chest.

"Well, back then I'd do a lot of shaving before a meet."

Having heard what Tristan had said, my mind couldn't help but think. With his hands and feet, he probably raced through the water like a damn torpedo. I know it sounds crass but anyone seeing his hands and feet would think the same thing. Maybe his birth defect became a plus instead of a negative in his life. And don't get me wrong. They didn't detract from his incredibly handsome good looks at all. Hell no. It made me realize there was no need to even address the issue. He was comfortable with himself and that's all that mattered.

He looked over at me. "What about you?"

I snickered. "I was never any good at any sport. The closest I got was being the school mascot in college."

During the telling of his history, he, too, had made no mention of some significant person in his life. I guess he was straightforward when he said he hadn't met the right one. He did mention several good friends but there was never mention of someone special. It was totally surprising to me, how someone as good-looking as he was could escape the clutches of someone. True, I'd just met this man and only chatted with him for a few hours but he seemed to have a very nice personality, was sincere and easy to get along with. From his reaction to some of my comments, it was obvious he also had a good sense of humor.

I began to think about all I had heard. Both of us had just met, so there would be no reason we'd display all of our cards on the table. I'm sure we both had things we weren't ready to express to the other. I know I did.

"How is it that a man from Atlanta is here on the southwest coast of Mexico? To me, that's a major stretch." He was very curious.

"What can I say? You're absolutely correct. It began with an article in an architectural magazine. And I know you're going to laugh but it also has something to do with what I was told by an old gypsy lady."

He looked at me with a major questioning expression. "You're kidding me, aren't you? I can understand the influence of an article in a magazine but an old gypsy lady?"

"Seriously. And what's really freaky is it was the same one over and over for something like a twenty..." I paused for a moment, tilted my head back, calculating it in my mind. "Yes. Twenty-four. A twenty-four-year period of time."

Tristan was amazed. "No. You have to be joking. Over twenty-four years and it was the same gypsy lady? What are the chances of that happening?"

"I know. And after the first time when I was ten, she recognized me and knew who I was every time. Even with the time between each session, it seemed like the conversation just picked up where the last one left off."

I paused for a moment remembering. "The last time I saw her was just about four years ago. It was rather sad. We both realized we'd never see each other again in this life. I know this is going to sound incredibly bizarre but I felt like I was saying goodbye to a favorite aunt. It even affected Nick, too. I was somewhat surprised at how much it affected him. Not to say Nick doesn't have a heart. But he was only witnessing the sessions. She wasn't reading his fortune." I paused for a moment. "But that's really not quite true, either. She kept saying his and my Destiny were connected."

"I must admit. That's rather incredible. What kind of information did she give you?"

"She kept telling me my Destiny would be found in the sea. And it would happen in my late thirties. Well. I'm thirty-seven now. Will be thirty-eight in June. Sure is getting close, isn't it? One thing very interesting though is she couldn't see anything, regarding my life beyond that point. Her comment was something like there was a wall, blocking her from seeing any farther. She did indicate there was nothing there, regarding death. I was supposed to find real happiness there but she couldn't elaborate."

"Humm. That IS interesting. I'm surprised you put credence in it. I believe most people have no belief in that stuff." Tristan shook his head.

"Believe me. I know there are lots of charlatans out there but this lady was totally different. She had a sincerity, an honesty about her. I can't explain it. And things she did tell me when I was very young, did come to pass."

"Really? Like what?"

I realized immediately without thinking, I'd opened the door I hadn't intended to so soon. I didn't want him to know I wasn't like a lot of other guys. It could possibly make him feel uncomfortable. "Well. Ah. It was just some personal stuff." I stared down at the table, not wanting to look directly at him. I was afraid if he could look in my eyes, he'd see me. The real me inside. The one I was hiding from him.

"I'm sorry. I didn't mean to pry." He reached across the table with his right hand and patted the top of mine, sitting on the table. He looked at me and smiled. "So, you're an architect and an artist. Do you have any of your artwork here? It has always amazed me how people can take paint and make it actually look like something you could almost reach in and pick up or touch. I jokingly tell people, I can't draw a straight line." He gave a big smile.

"I think there are about six of my paintings, hanging here in the house. Nick has a few in his house, too. Come on. I'll show them to you."

We got up and walked through the house as I showed him several oil paintings, hanging on the walls of the living room and dining room. His response was always very positive. We walked over to Nick's, so he could see those then back over to my house and out on the terrace.

I called out as I headed into the house. "I did say we'd have a Bloody Mary, didn't I? Let me fix us one."

Bringing out the two drinks, I handed one to Tristan. He took a sip. "I swear. This is really good and refreshing. You should open a bar."

This had us both laughing before the conversation returned to the subject at hand.

"I know you were planning to spend your time on the beach but I do hope you brought more clothes with you because it should be quite obvious none of mine will fit you." I pulled at my shirt.

"Yes. Yes, I did. Not many as I had no intention of doing anything except relaxing for a week."

Realizing the physical condition of his hands and feet, my heart began to hurt again for him. Of course, he wouldn't be strolling through town or seeing any sites. I'm sure he didn't want people just constantly staring at him. It is sad. Why are we like that? We see something different and immediately we stare or reject it. It's terribly sad.

Suddenly, an episode of the old 'Twilight Zone' TV series came into my head. It was the one where the lady was having plastic surgery done on her face, so she would look normal like everyone else. But when they take the bandages off, her face is still the same. There had been no change. You hear everyone in the room call out. "There's no change!" And here's the twist. She, as the viewer perceives her, is beautiful. But then you finally see the people of that society. As the viewer sees them, they are ugly. It's the old expression. 'Beauty is in the eye of the beholder.' And I believe the name of the episode was 'Eye of the Beholder'.

I loved Rod Serling and his 'Twilight Zone' episodes. The episodes made you think. They also addressed many social issues.

He was truly an incredibly talented and creative man. A man ahead of his time.

Tristan looked at me questioningly. "What is wrong? I see anguish on your face."

I shook my head. "It's people. Sometimes people just annoy me. They're constantly judging a book by its cover."

"Wow. Something really powerful did go through your head for you to come out with that comment." A warm smile came to his face. "Don't worry about things you have no control over. You can work toward change but it doesn't happen overnight. And sometimes, it doesn't happen at all."

I looked right into his wonderful blue eyes. "You know. You are absolutely correct. Sounds like you went to the same twelve-step program I did." I immediately began recalling those evenings, sitting with several others, regarding my codependency.

I quickly changed the subject. "Let me see what I have to fix for dinner. The freezer in the refrigerator isn't very big. And I wasn't expecting company so soon." I looked at Tristan and smiled. "But I will say, I'm really glad to have you here."

Tristan smiled back. "Thank you. Thank you, very much. I, too, am glad we have met."

I went to the kitchen and checked the freezer. I yelled out. "How do steaks or pork chops on the grill sound?"

"Hey! I'm just visiting. You pick whatever you want." He called back.

"Okay. Steaks it is." I pulled a zip plastic bag with two steaks in it out of the freezer and placed them in the sink to thaw. I ran some cold water into the sink to speed the process. When they were ready, I'd put them back in the refrigerator again with some nice Worcestershire sauce marinade. "How about a refill on your Bloody Mary?"

"Sounds good. Let me bring you my glass." Tristan came into the kitchen for a refill. "How about a walk on the beach after finishing our drinks?"

"That sounds great. Let me get you some sunscreen, so you don't burn." After handing him his Bloody Mary, I went into the main bathroom closet and got out the squeeze bottle of sunscreen. I returned to the terrace as Tristan was already out there. He had removed his T-shirt, putting it on one of the chairs.

I walked over to him. "Here. Set your glass down on the table and hold out your arms." I squeezed some of the lotion in my hands and started rubbing it all over his back. Then, I rubbed some on his shoulders. "I think that has it." I smiled.

He turned and looked at me with a big grin. "But what about the rest of me?" He flexed his eyebrows several times. "I can just tell. I'll bet you give a great back rub. Oh, yeah."

I shook my head with a big grin on my face. "Don't tempt me. And I just might not stop with your back." I handed him the squeeze bottle of sunscreen. I have to admit, I was very curious as to whether he meant his comment as a joke or was he trying to tell me something. I might have to question him about it later on when I felt more comfortable to do so.

Tristan took the bottle of sunscreen and began applying it over the rest of his body. "Okay. I think that does it. Now, we can go for a walk on the beach."

I took the bottle from him and applied some on myself. We finished our drinks and I smiled. "Okay. Let's go."

As we walked north up the beach, our conversation was basically small talk, regarding things. He told me how much he liked the ocean, the arts, music. And I responded accordingly. We had been out for a little over two hours when we were back near the house again.

"Let's run in and I'll fix a jug of iced tea to take with us. I can also marinate the steaks and put them in the refrigerator."

We must have walked another hour down the beach, stopping periodically to have a drink of tea. I have always liked the tea I make. Half black and half green. When it's done, I add lemon, sugar and an apple juice I found in the grocery store here in Mexico. Gives the tea a nice flavor.

I couldn't believe how easy and comfortable it was to be with Tristan. We talked a little about his questioning of himself, regarding the responsibilities in front of him. From the way it sounded, the business he was supposed to take over was quite large and had many, many employees. There were never any details as to the kind of company it was. It really didn't matter as it was none of my business. Regardless, it definitely had him stressed out. I could only imagine the pressure he was under. Knowing he had traveled a long way just to think about it and contemplate the situation, made it obvious it was affecting him greatly. I don't know what I'd do if I were told to take over the architectural company I worked for. And it was no huge company.

I could see Tristan was around my own age. I can only imagine his parents were probably constantly concerned about the fact he wasn't married yet. Was it really that important? Geez. It was obvious to me and quite doubtful I would ever marry unless legal systems changed. I didn't see that happening anytime soon. Yes. It was nineteen ninety-eight and many things have been changing in recent years but marriage was on the distant horizon. I was sure I would never live to see it.

After a while, we headed back to the house. All the tea had been consumed and it was getting close to dinner time. Tristan fired up the grill and before long, steaks and salad were on the table. When dinner was over, we went into the living room to sit and relax. Since Tristan liked my tea, I poured us a glass from the new batch I'd mixed up in a big container in the refrigerator.

Before I could sit down, Tristan asked if I would play something on the piano. I turned to him. "I sure as hell hope you're not expecting concert quality here. Vladimir Horowitz or Ashkenazy, I'm not." I grinned as I walked to the piano.

"So. What would you like to hear? And remember, my repertoire is very limited." Sitting on the bench, I turned to the right and smiled in his direction.

"Play whatever you like. I know I will enjoy it."

I began with a piece of Debussy, then a piece of Chopin and finally, *The Eighteenth Variation* by Rachmaninoff. After a moment, I turned to Tristan and said. "This last piece is a more modern one, especially compared to the Masters." Pausing, my voice became somewhat melancholy. "But I like to play it in memory of the friends I have lost in the past. There have been so many."

After a moment of silence, I played the introduction and began singing with the piano as an accompaniment in a slow and easy tempo, suitable for the song. "'I'll be seeing you... in all the old familiar places... that this heart of mine embraces... all day through.'" I continued, trying to sing and play with all the emotion the song evokes. As the smiling faces of my many dead friends passed through my mind, tears began to roll down my cheek and a slight crack came to my voice.

Finally, the song was coming to its end. "'I'll see you in the morning sun... and when the night is new... I'll be looking at the moon... but I'll be seeing...... you.'" I held the last word as the final broken chords moved up the piano keyboard to a pianissimo and then the ending chord in the lower register of the piano.

As the sound faded away, I turned my head to the left, so Tristan wouldn't see my tears. Getting up from the bench, I turned to the left, so I could wipe my eyes with my right hand. I walked over to sit down near Tristan but stopped short when I saw his face.

He was looking right up at me, silent. Tears were streaming down and his face was filled with sadness. He whispered. "That is such a beautiful song. But it is SO SAD when you put it in the context of remembering people you have lost. My heart aches for you and I feel your pain. I can tell how meaningful that song is to you. I'm so sorry." He stood up, walked over and wrapped his arms around me, pulling me close.

I wrapped my arms around him, placing my head on his upper

chest. We stood there silent for several minutes, rocking back and forth. It was comforting to be held by him.

Eventually, sitting down, Tristan looked at me. "You are young. How is it you could have lost so many friends? Did you have friends a lot older than yourself?"

At that moment, I realized I couldn't keep the door closed any longer. I had to lay all my cards on the table and let Tristan in on what I had been trying to avoid. "Tristan. No. They were not older. They were men. Men my own age. Some younger and some older."

From the expression on his face, I could see the wheels were turning in his mind. Finally, he spoke quietly. "Oh. I believe I understand. They were..." He paused for a second, looking down at the floor. Then, his head came up and he looked right at me. "They were... homosexuals? Gay men?"

"Correct." I was waiting for his reaction.

He bent his head down and spoke quietly. "The AIDS crisis. Yes." He paused for a moment then looked directly at me. "Do you mind if I ask you a very personal question?"

I knew the question coming and braced for it to be asked.

Tristan looked at me with caring eyes. "Are you..." He paused for a moment and looked down at the floor.

Before he could continue, I spoke. "Yes. Yes, I am. And I'm one of the lucky ones. I'm not sick. I'm fine." I waited to see his reaction.

He didn't even flinch. "I'm so sorry." He spoke softly and with sympathy. "Yes. We heard and knew about the crisis, hitting the gay community. But it has affected many, many heterosexual people as well."

He paused for a moment then bent his head down, staring at the floor again. "You have told me something very private about yourself. And to be honest, I am glad you have done so. Because..." He paused and was silent for a few moments before continuing. "Because. I am the same. That has been my struggle for so long. I have tried with great difficulty to hide it. I think you now understand my dilemma. I have had no one to talk to."

To say, I was shocked and astounded would be putting it mildly and a total understatement. I was incredibly stunned. What I couldn't understand is why he had no one to talk to. Immediately, it dawned on me. He was probably from a well-known family, moneyed and probably with influence. Stuck in that situation, it would be very difficult to talk with anybody. Because sure enough, your secret would be out and all over the place. That's why he had to keep it under wraps. Many of my questions about him were instantly answered.

I spoke quietly. "Tristan. Oh, my God. I had no idea. I want you to know we can talk. Whatever you tell me will be in confidence. I would never divulge your secret. We can talk whenever you like. We can talk about anything and everything. Remember that."

He looked at me and smiled. "I have sensed you would be the kind of man I could talk to. But I wasn't sure how to approach it. The minute you opened the door, I knew it would be all right."

"Wow. I can see this is going to be some conversation. It's something you're probably wanting to talk about immediately. I don't want to sound like I'm trying to put you off but how about we do this. Since it's getting late, let's sleep on it. It will give you time to contemplate the kind of questions in your head. I have a feeling every question you ask will bring up more questions. Let's get a good night's rest and begin fresh in the morning. How does that sound?"

"That sounds like a terrific idea." He smiled.

As I turned out the light and got in bed, I could hear the roar of the ocean waves, crashing on the rocks down on the beach. I knew the next day was going to be a very interesting one.

CHAPTER IX

Needless to say, I was absolutely correct. The conversation for the entire morning was very interesting. We compared life experiences and of the times we were questioning ourselves and the wondering why. It was also quite funny when we started talking about the checklist in our heads of the physical qualities we found desirable.

"I think it goes back to old TV shows." I stared off into space, remembering. "Especially, the old cowboy shows. You bet. It was always the tall, dark and handsome ones that got me going. Especially, if they were furry with dark fur. Oh, yeah!"

Immediately, Tristan stood up and gave a muscleman pose. He looked at me and grinned. "You mean, someone like this?" Then, he stroked his furry chest with his right hand.

I bent my head down, shaking it. "I cannot tell a lie. Yes. Someone like you." I snickered. "Okay. Let's hear your checklist. I'll bet it's some tall blonde with blue eyes and built like a you-know-what."

Tristan sat down and smiled. "Well. You are teetotally wrong." He flexed his eyebrows.

A questioning look filled my face. "Really? I surely thought you would have gone for some cute, sexy blonde."

"Well. You're wrong. Totally wrong." He paused for a few moments. "I prefer someone that's about a head shorter than me. I also like dark hair. Average build. Not really into those that are heavyset."

I immediately jumped up and did the same muscleman pose he

did before. "Oh. You mean someone like this?" I started to laugh and couldn't stop.

He stood up and clapped his hands together. "Yes! You've got it! Someone just like you!" He grinned. "Come over here, you silly goose."

When I did, he grabbed me and held me close. I can't explain how comfortable it felt.

After a few moments, I pulled away and smiled. "Okay. We have chatted the whole morning away. We have to do something for dinner tonight. Since you're such a great swimmer, why don't you take your raft out and see if you might be able to find a couple of lobsters, crawling around under the ocean in those rocks offshore."

"You know? That sounds like a terrific idea. We can have them for dinner tonight. I'll head out right now."

I added. "If you don't see any, not to worry. I'll find something here."

We walked down to the beach, bringing Tristan's raft. It was much lighter with nothing in it. As I watched, Tristan dragged his raft into the surf. I realized he would probably be out there for some time. Returning to the house, I went to the other guest room and set up my easel. I was going to paint. And what was I going to paint? Well. Let's just say I'm going to tell him it's a sunset over the ocean. Actually, I'll paint one of those as well. I set up my second easel.

It didn't take me long to set everything up and get the initial background colors on both the canvases. Checking the time, I had a feeling he'd be returning shortly. So, I took two pieces of cloth and covered the canvases to keep any dust from getting in the paint.

Getting to the beach, I could see him several hundred feet offshore. I waved my arms in the air.

He responded similarly, grabbed the paddle and started ashore. Soon, he landed and pulled the raft up onto the beach. He reached in the raft and held up two lobsters, one in each hand.

I ran over to him. "Let me have those and you can drag the raft up to the house."

As I reached and took the lobsters, he looked at me strangely. "What's that on your face?" He rubbed his right hand on his bathing suit and then touched my face. "It's paint. You're painting. Wow. When did you start that?"

"Oh. Just after you launched the raft. I got it going and I have the background colors in already. It's going well."

"I think that's great. What are you painting?"

"Thought I would do a sunset. They are so beautiful here." I hadn't told a lie. I was truly painting a sunset.

"Can I see it?"

"No. No one ever sees one of my paintings until it's finished. And before you ask, when? I think it will take some time. Hopefully, before I have to go back to Atlanta. But I may have to stay up a little late at night to work on it." I looked at the lobsters. "Okay. Let's get these babies cooking."

After dinner, we talked a little more. I played a few more pieces on the piano and then it was time to head to bed.

As Tristan opened his bedroom door, he looked at me and smiled. "See you in the morning."

"In the morning." Instead of heading to my room, I went to the other guest bedroom and did some more painting for a little over two hours. Both paintings were turning out very well. Slow, but well. As I placed a cloth over each one, I smiled.

With breakfast over the next day, Tristan decided to go out in the raft again and do some fishing. "Maybe I can catch us a nice red snapper."

"That would be fantastic. We can cook it on the grill. I have a screen, so it won't fall through the rungs. I'll also fix a salad."

While he was out fishing, I did some more work on the paintings. They were shaping up fairly well but they were going to take some time.

I watched Tristan return from the sea. I was amazed at his agility in the water. He had caught a beautiful red snapper. Fortunately, he'd brought with him a fish scaler and fillet knife. He said he knew he'd need them if he was going to live from the ocean while he was here. It made perfect sense. It was incredible how he managed the fish. It was like watching one of those TV cooking shows on the Public Broadcasting System channel.

Before we headed into the living room after dinner, I asked. "How would you like a nice Whiskey Sour?"

Tristan smiled. "If they are as good as your Bloody Marys, I'd love one."

I had a jug of them already made in the refrigerator and poured us each a glass. Heading back to the living room again, I handed one to Tristan.

He took a sip. "Yep! You definitely need to open a bar."

We both roared with laughter.

After we calmed down, I spoke quietly. "Tristan. I've thought so much about your situation and I truly understand. I wish I could give you some advice on a path to take but I'm sorry. This is a road only you can choose. You know the consequences of your choice most of all."

He bent his head down. "Yes. You're right. I just have to make up my mind and take action."

I looked at him with caring eyes. "I hope you don't mind me asking as I don't want to muddy the water. Is there anyone you have thought about who you would consider as your partner? If there is, maybe you could discuss this with him and see if he's willing to live in such a way there was no blatant display you were together. I know that's not fair but life isn't fair."

"No. There isn't. Of all those I have met and know, none of them are ones I could care about much less love. All they see is my position and all it involves. They don't see me. I want to have someone who loves me for me and not my position and family. It's one reason I've never been able to even engage someone even for fun."

I looked at him with great surprise. "Are you telling me in your entire life, you have never been with someone?"

He bent his head down, nodding it. "Correct."

"Tristan. That's such a shame. I do understand your situation. But again, it's such a shame you haven't experienced anything physical with another person. You truly are in a dilemma. Damn. And I just know you would make love with someone in a very passionate way. It's sad."

Finally, we ended the conversation and headed off to bed. We expressed 'goodnight's and headed to our rooms.

Instead of going to my room, I decided to do more work on the paintings. As I did, I found myself thinking about Tristan. His handsome face was in my head. I thought of the conversations we'd had. It was such a shame such a man should be so constrained with being who he was, he was unable to have a physical experience with another. I could tell he would be a man who'd be loving and caring. It would be a tragedy for him never to find someone special and never have loved the way he wanted to love.

But I did realize the problems of being from a family of prominence and means as well as owning a big and important company. Especially, if he was supposed to take it over. What would the backlash be from employees and top executives who might not agree with his orientation? That kind of situation could destroy the company. And then, there were the gold diggers out there.

It was sad. No wonder he wanted to get far away and think. It was a shame he had no siblings to take over the company. That way he could step back and advise from the background. But that was not an option.

I shook my head. "Such a shame." I whispered.

I stood back and looked at the two canvases. I was quite pleased with how they were coming along. I put the brush into the jar of turpentine, covered the canvases, headed to my room and got in bed.

Finally, the sound of the crashing surf put me to sleep.

CHAPTER X

The ringing of the satellite phone woke me up. I looked over at the alarm clock. It was six o'clock. I grabbed the phone, thinking it had to be an emergency. It was so expensive to make calls on it, Nick and I had agreed not to do it unless it was really important.

"Hello?"

"Hey, guy. It's me. I know it's early and I didn't want to run up a big charge, so I will make this quick. I wanted to call you before I left for work. Everything here has gone exceptionally well. My clients are super happy. Everything should be cleared up by the end of today. I'll make reservations and let you know what time I'll get there tomorrow. I know it's going to cost me an arm and a leg, making reservations so close to flight time but I don't care. I can't wait to get down there and enjoy all that wonderful paradise."

"Nick. Not to worry. Call me when you know. Call me anyway as I've got something to tell you. Something important."

"Oh, my God! You've met someone! I can just tell. I can feel it in your voice. You have, haven't you?"

I couldn't help myself and started to chuckle. "I swear to God! You amaze me sometimes. I can't believe someone knows me so well. I'll tell you later on. Now, go to work and get finished, so you can get down here."

"Okay. Hopefully, I'll see you tomorrow afternoon sometime. Later. Later."

"Bye."

I was glad Nick was going to be able to make it even though his vacation would be shorter. And I couldn't wait for him to know about Tristan.

I got out of bed. After getting dressed, I went to the kitchen and started breakfast. That's when I heard a noise out on the front terrace. I went to the sliding screen door and looked out, seeing Tristan sitting at the table. I opened the door. "Are you all right? Sitting out there in the dark. Let me turn on the lights."

Tristan smiled. "I'm fine. I woke up very early and decided to come out to just enjoy the breeze and the peace here."

"I'll have breakfast for us in a few minutes and coffee."

"That sounds really great. Thank you. I don't know how I'll ever repay you."

"Don't be ridiculous. When friends are visiting me, I don't charge them to stay. They are my friends. And now, I consider you one of my friends."

"Well, I want you to know I truly appreciate your friendship and kindness as well as all this wonderful food and drink you're serving me."

"I just want you to have a good time. That's what this place is all about." I paused for a moment. "I just got a call from Nick. He says he should be finished with everything up there and is planning to take the first flight out tomorrow. He should be here by tomorrow afternoon. I can't wait for you to meet him."

"You have phone service out here?"

"Nick and I have a satellite phone right now. It's expensive as all get out to make a call but we don't use it that often. There will be cell phone service down the road. I guess not enough demand yet to build a tower out this way."

"Are you sure I won't be in the way?"

"Don't worry. Nick's house is right next door. You being here is not a problem."

"Well. If you say so, that's terrific. How about while you're going to get Nick, I go out and catch us some nice lobsters for dinner?"

"I think that sounds like a terrific idea. You don't mind?"

"It's the least I can do." He gave a big smile.

"Terrific! Nick and I can stop by the store and stock up on groceries before heading back here." My mind understood. I believe one reason Tristan didn't want to go with me was due to his physical afflictions. I totally got it.

The sun was up for a while before heading out for a walk on the beach. I fixed us a large jug of iced tea to take with us. It was obvious how much Tristan enjoyed the ocean with the number of times he dove into the surf.

Returning to the house, he decided to go in and take a nap since he'd gotten up so early. I was glad as this gave me time to do more work on my paintings. I told him to sleep as long as he wanted. We were not on any specific time schedule.

For about two hours, I worked. Both were turning out very well. A few more hours and the sunset most likely would be completed. Before going to bed that night, I'd try to finish the task.

Nick also had called to confirm he'd be arriving the next day at around eleven in the morning. I was glad he was going to be able to make it. He was taking a late-night flight out of Atlanta, stay at the airport overnight in Mexico City then take the morning flight to Zihuatanejo.

When I went out to fix dinner, I saw Tristan was up from his nap and sitting out on the terrace. I called out to him. "Would you like some iced tea before dinner?"

"Thank you. I'd love some."

"I want you to feel free here. If you want to drink something or eat something, please, feel free to get it. What's the expression here? Mi casa es su casa."

After dinner, we sat out on the terrace just to chill and relax before heading to bed. When we did, I worked a few more hours on the paintings. The sunset one was ready for its frame but the other still needed a lot of work.

Since I had quite a few frames in storage under the staircase to the roof, I knew there would be one suitable for each one. As I rummaged through them, I saw it. "Perfect." I took it in and placed the canvas inside it. Setting it on the easel, I got to stand back and look at it. I was pleased. The colors in the sunset were wonderful but my ocean wasn't the best. Hey. I wasn't Winslow Homer. The frame helped it a lot. I have always said a frame can make or break a painting no matter how good or bad it is.

Lying in bed, I smiled. I knew exactly where I was going to hang each one in the living room. The sunset would be hung tomorrow.

CHAPTER XI

It was Thursday morning. I got up and started breakfast. Virtually at the same time, Tristan came out of his room. "Good morning." He smiled at me.

I smiled back. "Good morning to you. Breakfast and coffee in a few. But before I fix it, I want to set an anchor and screw in the wall in the living room."

Tristan gave a big smile. "Your painting. It's finished? I can't wait to see it. I'll bet it's a beautiful sunset."

"You can make that judgment when you see it. I'll probably hang it when I get back from picking Nick up at the airport."

Before I left, I told Tristan to feel at home. Get whatever he wanted or needed. "And be careful out there in those rocks. I don't want to get back here and find a drowned man on the beach. Got that? Now. Is there anything you need from town?"

"No. Not a thing. And don't worry. I'll be careful. See you later on this afternoon."

It was a little before eleven when I arrived at the airport. It gave me time to sit down and have a cup of coffee. Finally, there was an announcement of arrival. Eventually, I saw Nick's smiling face as he came through the doors from customs and immigration.

When he walked up, he placed his luggage on the floor and gave me a big hug. "Okay! I want to hear all about it. Or should I say… him." He looked around. "Where is he?"

I shook my head. "And hello to you, too. Geez."

Nick snickered. "Okay. Sorry. Hello!" He hugged me again. "It's just I'm so excited for you."

"Well. I'll get to that shortly. Let's get moving." We headed to the car.

Driving down the road, I began to tell him. "Nick. We're going to the grocery store before heading home. I want to make sure we have enough food for the time we're here." As we went, I started telling Nick more. "You're not going to believe it. It is totally strange. He came out of the sea."

"What!? Out of the sea? It's not Aquaman, is it!?" His mouth made a huge Cheshire Cat grin.

"Sometimes I swear! Just wait. Wait till you see him." I continued to explain about Tristan.

Nick was amazed at how Tristan appeared on the beach. "I'd have thought he was doing something with drugs as well. One question I have now is where is he from? Did he tell you where he came from?"

I bent my head down. "I did ask him in the beginning but all he said was that he was from far, far away."

"Ah. Excuse me! That doesn't answer the question."

"Yes, I know but I didn't want to push the issue with him. I thought he would eventually tell me when he was ready to. Please, don't pressure him. He has a lot on his plate, dealing with who he is. I want things to unfold slowly for him."

As the conversation continued, Nick was impressed at how well we seemed to be getting along together. "Hey! Remember that old gypsy lady we went to see? She told you. You would find your Destiny in the sea. Is it possible Tristan is your Destiny?" He slapped his thigh with his hand. "Hey! Could be!"

I continued to tell him all that had happened with the conversations I'd had with Tristan. Explaining virtually everything, I finally came to the last important piece of information. I spoke quietly. "Nick. He's deformed."

"Deformed?" His face took on a questioning expression.

"Yes. But let me explain. They must be birth defects. It's his feet and hands. His hands have skin between the fingers and his feet are kind of like flippers. You'll understand when you see them."

"Holy shit! It IS Aquaman!" Immediately, Nick broke into song. "'Be kind to your web-footed friends. For that duck may be somebody's mother.'" He started to laugh.

"I swear to God! I'll beat the shit out of you if you make an issue of it. He seems to be quite comfortable with it, so I have never said anything. I'm sure that's why he didn't want to come with me today. People would stare and look at him funny. But it definitely doesn't distract from how good-looking he is."

"Let me guess." Nick started stroking his beard with his left hand. "Tall, hunky and covered with dark hair. Including his face." He started giggling.

"You BITCH!" I couldn't help myself and started giggling. "You know me too well."

"Hey!" Then, he started singing the line of the Elton John, Dionne Warwick song. "'That's what friends are for.'" He paused for a moment. "Okay. Next big question. 'Enquiring minds want to know.' Have you done anything yet?"

I knew Nick up one side and down the other and had been waiting for this question to come up. "And the answer to your question is NO! Nick! I swear! You're totally incorrigible."

"Yes. But that's why you love me." He smiled. "Okay. But you knew I was going to ask." There was a questioning expression on his face. "But you met on Saturday night and here it is Thursday."

"Well. I think we're just taking our time."

Nick rolled his eyes. "Yeah. Sure." He continued. "I'm sure, having gotten to know him quickly and dismissed many questions you should have asked. There are a slew of questions that come to my mind. Like where exactly is he from? How in the hell could he be deformed as you said he is and no one knows? That kind of thing would be all over the news. And why would the parents of someone who has physical imperfections be concerned about him not marrying or having him take over a major business? Something's not right here."

He continued. "You said he came ashore in a raft. Well, he sure as hell didn't sail all the way from China in a raft. It had to be somewhere close. But you said he had traveled a long time from far, far away. True. In a raft, it would take a long time to go just a few miles in the ocean. Somehow, and I can't explain why but it sounds like he's from somewhere far off and very secluded. It seems that he must have money. If so, why is he in a raft and not a motorboat or a yacht for that fact? Why did he come in at night and not during the day? Yes. These are questions I can't believe you didn't ask."

"I know. I know. But really. It doesn't matter to me. It's not that important." I smiled. "It's possible he came down here by car, parked it in a lot or at a friend's house then took off in his raft. Maybe he just likes his raft instead of a motorboat. Or a yacht."

Nick's face twisted. "Okay. I guess. You're probably right. Maybe he did drive down and parked somewhere. Maybe the answers to those questions are really not that important to you. But they sure do raise a red flag for me."

He paused and changed the subject. "You said he was familiar with the shoreline here and he's right. This is a great place to get away from it all."

"And that's the point." I turned and looked at Nick with a stern expression. "As I've said. I think he has a lot on his plate. That's why he wanted to get away from everything. So. Don't stress him out with more questions. Right now, they are irrelevant."

"Okay. You've got it. No interrogations." Nick held up his hand. "I promise."

Finishing the shopping, we headed to the house. Nick took his things over to his house then came over to mine to help me put the groceries away. The minute he walked in he turned his head around sniffing. "You're painting! I can smell it."

"You have to be kidding me. Is the paint smell that strong? I mean, I do have the door closed to the room."

"Not to worry. It's not bad. It's just a small hint of turpentine in the air." He turned his head around again in a searching manner as if looking for something. "All right. I give up. Where are you hiding him?" He looked right at me. "Okay! He's not a blow-up doll you found floating in the ocean and you have it hidden in the bedroom?" He bent over, clapping his hands and started laughing.

"NICK! Good thing you're not close or I'd hit you with something. Damn!" I started laughing. "But. That was funny."

We both laughed out loud.

"He's out in the ocean. He wanted to catch some lobsters for dinner. I'll bet if we go out to the terrace, we'll be able to see him out in the raft." I paused for a moment. "But before we go out, I was hoping you'd help me hang a painting after we get the groceries put up."

"No sweat. So, it's ready? And where are you putting it?"

"I've already drilled a hole in the wall and set an anchor. All I have to do is have a little help getting a hanger wire on the screw. I didn't want to smear the paint."

"Cool. Let's do it."

We put the food away then walked into the second guest bedroom. I pulled the cloth off the framed canvas of the sunset. Nick stood, looking at the canvas with a big smile on his face. "Wow. That's not bad." Then, he looked over at the other covered canvas. "What's this?" He pointed.

"I'm doing another painting. It's not finished yet. I want to try and make it as perfect as possible."

"Can I look? I know you don't like folks to see your stuff until it's done. Just a peek?"

"Well. Okay." I reached over and removed the cloth.

Nick's mouth dropped open. "Wow! Holy shit! And you say it isn't done? It sure looks finished to me. Wow! I'm a straight guy but I have to admit. If that's a decent representation of what he looks like, he's one smoking handsome guy. It's a fantastic portrait. And knowing how good you are with paint, I'm sure it portrays him exceedingly well. Wow! And look at those blue eyes! They are incredibly intense. Wow!"

"I should have it finished in a few days. Then, we can hang it." I smiled. "So, you think it's good?"

"I haven't met the guy but if he looks like that, all I can say is Wow! Sorry, I said all those things about him." He stared at the painting.

I took the cloth and covered it again.

We took the sunset painting out to the living room and very carefully hung it in the place I had prepared for it. I was quite pleased with it.

Nick stood back, shaking his head. "Looks good. Looks good."

I looked at Nick. "He doesn't know about the portrait. I didn't want him to see it before it was time. So, don't say anything about it."

"No sweat. Mum's the word."

"Now. How about a glass of iced tea before we go sit on the terrace?"

"Sounds good to me."

I poured two glasses and we headed out onto the terrace. I looked out, scanning the ocean. Finally, I saw the raft and it was far out to sea. I squinted my eyes to try and see more clearly. I noticed Tristan was not in the raft. I had no idea why he would be out so far. "Maybe the lobsters were bigger out there." I muttered.

"What's the matter?"

"Just a thought crossing my mind. He never goes out that far when looking for lobsters. He usually gets them near the rocks closer to shore. He could be doing some fishing, though. He's got a great speargun. That could be it." I paused as several minutes went by. "Now, I know no one can hold their breath that long underwater. This does concern me."

Just as I spoke, we saw Tristan break the surface and climb into the raft. He grabbed a paddle and started heading toward shore.

"Let's run down to the beach and meet him." Nick stood up.

"That's a great idea. Let's go." I grabbed his arm. "And remember.

Don't stare at his hands and feet. I don't want him to feel awkward. And don't say anything about the painting, either."

"Not to worry. I get it. Chill."

We walked out and down to the beach where I anticipated Tristan to bring in the raft. It was the easiest path through the rocks.

As he got closer, he saw us and waved. I heard him call out. "I'll be there in a few minutes." Finally, reaching the shore, he jumped out of the raft and pulled it onto the beach. He stood up and walked over to us. He looked and smiled at Nick. "Hello. You must be Nick. Nice to meet you." He extended his hand and shook Nick's.

"Nice to meet you, Tristan." Nick smiled then turned to me and flexed his eyebrows several times.

I knew immediately what he was thinking. I just bent my head down to keep from snickering.

Tristan walked over to the raft. "I got us some very nice ones for dinner tonight." He reached in the raft and grabbed two of the lobsters, holding them up in the air. I took them from him as he reached back in the raft to get the third. "Let's head to the house." With his other hand, he grabbed the handle of the raft.

"Let me help." Nick reached down and grabbed the other handle to help drag the raft to the house.

They pulled the raft up onto the terrace as Tristan indicated he was going in to change into some dry clothes.

"I'll get dinner started in a little while. Thought we could have something to drink in the meantime." I grabbed Nick's and my glasses off the table, rinsed them out in the kitchen sink then poured three Whiskey Sours, taking them out to the table on the terrace.

Nick looked over at me and spoke quietly. "Damn. He's one handsome dude. Wow! Not to worry about your painting. It has him to a tee." He smiled. "Oh. And I sincerely apologize for the song I started earlier today before I met him. I have a feeling he's a totally cool guy. Even with his hands and feet." He grinned.

Shortly, Tristan came out and joined us.

"Tristan. You'll have to come over and see my house. This talented guy right here designed it for me." Nick stood up.

"I'd like that. We did go see the paintings you have there but I didn't get to see your whole house." Tristan stood up.

"Well, I guess I could join you." I smiled.

As we toured Nick's house, Tristan continued to make comments about how wonderful and open it was. He turned and smiled at me. "Maybe one day you'll have to design a house for me." He stopped short and paused for a moment. "Didn't you say you were going to hang your sunset painting when Nick arrived? You know I can't wait to see it."

Nick immediately jumped in. "Why yes. We hung it in the living room just before you came in from the sea. I helped hang it. It turned out exceedingly well. Let's go." Nick led the way as we went back over to the house, walked into the living room and stood in front of the painting.

Tristan smiled. "Wow! Look at those beautiful colors. I love it. It's a wonderful painting. You artists amaze me. What can I say?" He grabbed me and hugged me.

Nick chimed in. "I think this calls for a refill." He held his glass up in the air.

The rest of the day was spent sitting around, sipping our Whiskey Sours, talking and laughing. Nick rehashed several stories from our past. He also told parts of his loveless marriage. "I tell you now. Make sure you love the person you marry for who that person is and not what they look like. Believe me. I thought Jenny was so hot, married her then realized I didn't know a thing about her. We had absolutely nothing in common. Nothing, except sex. I'm just glad we had no kids."

I entered the conversation. "I've always believed Destiny sometimes has a hand in who we should truly be with. I know that may sound crazy but I do."

"Are you referring to that old gypsy lady? I do have to admit. It was very strange." Nick looked into space in remembering the past.

Tristan smiled. "Yes. We have talked about the old gypsy lady in his past. I found it most interesting that it was always the same one over so many years."

"You've got that right." Nick was firm. "She kept saying he would find his Destiny in the sea. She never said what it would be but it wouldn't be anything bad."

Tristan shook his head. "I must admit, I find that very interesting as well. I can understand why you might believe her. Especially, with it being the same woman every time."

Nick spoke up. "But there was something about her that made you believe her. An honesty. A sincerity. You just knew she was telling the truth."

I added. "Well, Destiny better hurry up and get its ass in gear as I'm not getting any younger. Two more years and it'll be over. What can I say?"

After dinner, the conversation was light. Soon, it was time to go to bed.

"Okay, guys. I'm heading over to the house. See you all in the morning." Nick stood up and headed off the terrace. "Tristan. Great to meet you, guy. I think you're totally cool."

Tristan smiled. "Nick! Nice to meet you as well."

"Come on over for omelets in the morning." I called out.

"Okay. Sounds good to me. What time?" Nick called out.

"Whenever you get here. Omelets are a snap to make." I responded.

Nick yelled out from the dark. "Later. Later."

Tristan and I walked into the kitchen. As I turned to head to the bedroom, Tristan grabbed my arm and dragged me into the living room. We were standing in front of the painting.

"It is a fine work. Maybe someday I'll have you paint a picture for me." He smiled. "And all you have done for me. I can never repay you."

I looked up into Tristan's face. "Friends never owe friends." I smiled.

Tristan grabbed me and gave me a big hug. As he held me close, he whispered in my ear. "May I be with you tonight?"

I looked up into his face and smiled. I reached up with both hands and pulled his head down toward mine and kissed him passionately. After a few moments, I pulled away, looking into his eyes. "Does that answer your question?"

We both smiled as I grabbed his hand and led him to my bedroom.

CHAPTER XII

The next morning was Friday and we were awakened by the sound of Nick's voice. "Hello. Are you up yet? Are we still having omelets this morning?"

I lifted my head from the pillow and called out. "We'll be out in a few."

"No problem. I'll give you guys about twenty minutes and then I'll be back over here."

I turned and looked into Tristan's smiling face. "I'm sorry. I had no idea we slept so late."

"Not to worry. And thank you for last night. It meant a great deal to me. I must tell you. It was wonderful to feel you close to me. I had no idea it would be so amazing."

I smiled at him. "Yes. Yes, it was. I have never experienced such with another. Thank you for being with me." I paused for a few seconds. "Well, we better get up. Nick will be back over here and please ignore the lecherous look that will be on his face. He is surely going to know we slept together last night. And if he says anything smart, I'm going to pop him upside the head."

We both were laughing as we got out of bed.

I believe you could set a watch by Nick's punctuality. No sooner had we walked out into the kitchen than he was knocking on the sliding glass door again. "Oh! I see you're up. Both of you." A huge grin filled his face. He flexed his eyebrows several times.

I looked at him sternly. "No comments from the Peanut Gallery. And, 'Enquiring minds' are NOT going to know."

That comment made everyone break out into raucous laughter.

Tristan asked while shaking his head. "You used the term 'Peanut Gallery'. I don't understand."

I just smiled. "I was talking with a friend of mine one time and he used that expression. I didn't understand it, either. Now, mind you, my friend at the time was in his early fifties and this was several, several years ago. He told me of an old kids' television show he used to watch when he was young. It was called 'The Howdy Doody Show'. The main character, Howdy Doody, was a puppet. Actually, a marionette. The real live characters in the show were Buffalo Bob, Chief Thunderthud, Clarabell the Clown and Princess Summerfall Winterspring. And the live audience of children was called the Peanut Gallery because the kids were young. My friend said he and many of his peers used to use the expression when referring to a lot of people gathered together. And one more interesting tidbit of knowledge. The guy who used to play Clarabell the Clown was the same one who was Captain Kangaroo on TV. And we remember 'Captain Kangaroo', don't we? Now. Did that enlighten everyone?"

Nick looked up and rolled his eyes. "Oh. Sure. Yeah. Believe it!"

We all broke into more laughter.

It was mid-afternoon while we were sitting on the terrace when all of a sudden there came a low rumbling sound and everything began to shake. Within a few seconds, the sound got louder and the shaking more intense.

Tristan jumped up and yelled out. "Get out from under this tile roof! Run out onto open ground!"

Nick and I jumped up and we all ran out from under the roof of the terrace. The shaking was such that I ended up falling on the ground. It lasted some twenty seconds and was over.

I quickly jumped up and started jiving and dancing around, singing Carole King's song. "'I feel the earth... move... under my feet. I feel the sky tumbling down...'"

Everyone was laughing.

Nick jumped up and down, clapping his hands together and yelling. "YeeeHaw! I just experienced my first earthquake. I need to remember this. Friday, May the eighth, nineteen ninety-eight. I love it! My first earthquake."

Tristan just shook his head. "I'm so glad you two can take this so lightly. Earthquakes are serious things."

I quickly looked around. "You know? You're right. I think we need to check and see if there's any damage to the houses. Nick, let's go check yours first."

We all headed quickly over to Nick's house and began our inspection. After checking all the rooms, the walls, the ceilings and the floors, we saw no visible damage to Nick's house. Next, we headed back over to my house and did the same.

I called out. "Nick. Could you check the two guest bedrooms and main bathroom while Tristan and I check the master bedroom and bath? I'd appreciate it."

After doing all the checking, we saw there appeared to be no physical damage to mine, either.

Nick yelled out. "Got to tell you. I didn't expect any damage as this man knows his trade. Probably one of the best architects on the planet. You should have seen the foundations going in on these houses. Okay! I don't know about anyone else but this definitely calls for a drink. Hey! 'It's five o'clock somewhere.'"

We all agreed as I went to fix three Bloody Marys.

While we were standing on the terrace, I looked out to sea. "I think we need to watch the ocean for a while just to make sure we don't see any tidal wave coming in."

My comment seemed to disturb Tristan. He quickly stood up, pulled off his T-shirt, throwing it onto his chair, grabbed the corner of his raft and headed hurriedly to the beach. He called back. "I'll be right back in a little while. I need to check on something."

We watched as he raced into the surf, climbed into the raft and started paddling furiously out to sea.

Nick's face took on a questioning expression. "Okay. I give up. What's that all about? He didn't even take time to put on his bathing trunks."

I turned and looked at Nick. "I have no idea. You're as much in the dark as I am. I did hear him say he needed to check on something. What the hell is he checking on out there in the ocean?"

Nick and I sat down at the table and began to drink our cocktails. We watched Tristan paddle far out beyond the rock formations. After a few moments, he placed the paddle in the raft. He threw the small anchor into the water to hold the raft in place. Then, we watched him dive into the water. Several minutes went by and we didn't see Tristan return to the surface. We watched more closely.

Nick spoke softly. "I realize with hands and feet like his, he has to be a great swimmer but I don't know of anyone who can hold their breath that long underwater."

"I was thinking the same thing. No. Not about his hands and feet but holding his breath."

As time ticked by, I became very concerned. "Maybe I should run down and see if I can see him."

Nick spoke out again. "I think you can see better from here. Maybe he has come up to the surface behind some rock formation. That's why we haven't seen him."

I shook my head. "I guess you could be right. I just hope he's all right."

Nick shook his head. "I'm sure he knows what he's doing. He doesn't strike me as a dimwit."

We watched for some thirty minutes. Then, all of a sudden, Tristan broke the surface and climbed into the raft. He pulled up the anchor, grabbed the paddle and started slowly directing the raft toward the shore. In about ten minutes, he jumped out, pulled the raft out of the surf and headed to the house.

As he pulled the raft up onto the terrace, he turned to us with a big smile on his face, shaking his head. "Sorry about that. But I had to check on things and make sure everything was all right. Quakes are a funny thing. If you don't prepare for them, they can cause a lot of damage. Let me go change into something dry." He headed into the guest bedroom where all his things were located.

Nick and I were clueless. Of course, I had no idea exactly what he was talking about. And from the squirrelly expression on Nick's face, I knew he didn't, either.

When Tristan returned and joined us at the table, Nick looked directly at him. "What the hell was that all about? What is out there you had to check on? All we see is the deep blue sea."

Surprise filled Tristan's face. "Oh!" He began to snicker. "That's right. I forgot. I have never told you. You have no idea. It's my boat. It's anchored out there and I had to make sure it was secure. I also had to make sure everything in it was all right."

Nick raised both his hands in the air. "Okay! Wait a minute! I hate to say it but I don't see any boat out there. Is it invisible?" He started to chuckle. "Come on, now."

We all started to laugh.

"No. No. You can't see it because it's not on the surface. It's under the water." Tristan continued laughing.

Nick slapped his hand on the table. "You have to be shitting me! Well, I have to admit. That answers several questions I've had from the beginning. Something told me you came from far off and not from anywhere local. I knew you couldn't have used your raft to come from your original location. A submarine would make a whole hell of a lot of sense. I think that's SO totally awesome! You came here in a submarine." He paused slightly and looked directly at Tristan. "Is it yellow?"

Nick and I looked at one another and broke into raucous laughter. Somehow, it seemed Tristan didn't get the joke.

Still snickering I looked at Tristan. "The Beatles. Their song called *Yellow Submarine*. You know." I started singing the first line. "'We all live in a yellow submarine.... a yellow submarine..... a yellow submarine.'"

Tristan's face was filled with surprise. "Oh. Of course. How could I forget the Beatles?" He shook his head and joined the laughter.

I did find it interesting he traveled in a submarine and not in a boat on the surface. Knowing this, I still had no idea what kind of questions to ask. But it did clear up a question in my head, regarding the time before when he'd disappeared under the water for such a long period. He'd most likely gone down to his submarine to check on things. I thought it best to just let it pass for the present.

This was not the case for Nick. He spoke right up. "I think it's totally cool you have your own submarine. Since you don't seem to be upset, I assume everything's all right down there. But I'd think they were a lot more expensive to maintain than a boat that floats on the surface."

Tristan smiled. "To be honest, it's not my submarine. It's the one my family uses sometimes when they're traveling."

Nick smiled and clapped his hands together. "Wow! Totally, totally cool! A family that travels in a submarine on their vacations. Wow! YeeeHaw!!"

With dinner over, it again became time to go to bed. Nick waved as he headed toward his house. "See you guys in the morning."

As Tristan and I headed toward the bedrooms, Tristan looked at me and smiled. "Would it be all right if I was with you again tonight?"

I smiled, grabbed his hand and we headed into the bedroom.

It was Saturday morning. The sound of Nick at the door woke us both up.

I called out from bed. "Okay. Okay. We'll be up in a few minutes. Get the coffee started if you don't mind."

We heard Nick's response. "Will do. See you guys shortly. You want me to start breakfast?"

I yelled out. "Not to worry. We'll be out in a few." I turned to Tristan who was looking up at me. "Nick really is a cool guy. You've just got to love him."

Tristan smiled. "He really is. I understand why you both are friends. He is a true and genuine individual. You are very lucky to have someone like him as your friend."

We both got out of bed, dressed and headed to the kitchen.

Nick looked at us with a big smile. "Good morning, guys. Hope you both slept well." A sly look was on his face along with a huge Cheshire Cat grin.

Tristan nodded his head in the affirmative. "We slept very well. Thank you."

After a moment of silence, we all began to laugh.

As we were eating breakfast, Nick turned to Tristan. "How long are you here for?"

"I was planning to be here only a week but had no idea all this was going to happen. And since it has, it has given me a lot to think about. My life has finally taken a new direction and I'm glad of it."

I looked at Tristan and smiled. "So, you're going to stay a little longer? Great! I was hoping you would."

Tristan smiled. "I was hoping you'd be glad I was staying a little longer and didn't mind."

CHAPTER XIII

The next several days were spent just having a good time and enjoying the vacation. We were having such a good time, I didn't get to work on the portrait.

Every single day I became closer and closer to Tristan. I enjoyed his company and the times we spent together. The closer it got to going home, the more I hated the thought. Even Nick was fond of Tristan and was glad to see the closeness the two of us shared. But I knew that soon, we all had to return to our regular lives.

It was Thursday afternoon and we were sitting on the terrace, enjoying some iced tea and talking. I happened to be looking out to sea. Suddenly, out beyond the rock formations, I saw a group of figures rise from the water. I pointed. "What is that?" I quickly stood up.

This totally shocked Nick and he quickly stood up.

Tristan stood up and shook his head. He spoke quietly. "Damn. They found me."

Immediately, Nick and I looked at Tristan.

"You know who they are?" Nick was surprised.

"Yes. Yes, I do. I guess there is no escape." Tristan sat down.

Nick spoke in an alarming voice. "Escape? You're a criminal? An axe murderer!?"

I looked at Nick. "No. That's my line." I looked at Tristan. "You're an axe murderer!"

After a few seconds, we all laughed, knowing it wasn't true. But we were absolutely curious and very interested in what was going on.

Tristan continued looking out at the individuals in the ocean as they all began swimming toward shore. "No. No. Not a criminal. Definitely NOT an axe murderer. But it may be criminal for what I did. Sit down and I'll explain a little before they get up here."

Nick and I sat down and looked at Tristan.

Tristan spoke quietly. "I left without telling anyone. That is somewhat of a criminal act. I can't believe they found me. I turned off the homing device in the sub. But they're very, very good at their job. Yes. They've come to take me back. I know my parents are NOT going to be happy." He pounded his fist on the table. "But now. I know what I want. I know what I'm going to do." He turned and looked at me. "And I have you to thank for that. You have changed my life and helped me see and understand I cannot run away from myself."

We looked to the beach. There were around ten who had come out of the water. They were wearing the same deep blue-colored bathing suits but started shaking all over and shaking their heads of hair, trying to remove as much of the water as possible. When they were finally finished, they started heading to the terrace. We stood up and waited.

As they arrived, both Nick and I saw their hands and feet. All were like Tristan's. This made me wonder if they were from some colony of people all with the same deformity. Neither of us said a word.

Reaching the terrace, they seemed to get into a formation similar to a military group. They stood there for a moment, looking at Tristan. Then, with their right hands, they pounded their chest with their fist over their hearts. At that, they all went down on their right knees.

The leader of the group was a tall, well-built man, looking to be in his early fifties with a full beard and mustache of gray and white hair. The hair on his head was short and dark, sprinkled with gray. He looked up at Tristan, smiled and spoke quietly. "Your Highness!" They all bowed their heads and were silent.

Tristan spoke. "Togar. You and your men. Rise. Please."

Togar and the others stood. He spoke with a big smile on his face. "Your Highness. The quake did confuse the issue for a while. But. Did you really think you could give us the slip?"

Tristan bent his head down, shaking it. "Togar. You and your men are excellent at what you do. I knew sooner or later you'd probably find me."

I stood there with my mouth wide open at hearing 'Your Highness'.

Nick chimed in loud and clear. "Okay! Okay! Excuse me! A little info here!" He paused for only a moment. "'Your Highness'?? 'Enquiring minds want to know!'"

Nick's question broke my shock and I spoke. "Gentlemen. Please. Have a seat. Let me get more chairs."

Togar spoke up again. "But, Sire. It would not be befitting for us to sit..."

Tristan immediately cut him off. "Togar. Don't be ridiculous. You and your men will join us here and sit with us. You are fine men and I have the greatest respect for all of you. Certainly, you should be sitting and enjoying time with us. These are two fine men and I want you to treat them the same you would me."

Togar bowed his head toward Tristan. "Thank you, Your Majesty. That is very kind of you."

Nick spoke again. "Let me go get the ones off my terrace. Maybe a few tables, too. Togar, if you and some of the guys could help, we can get enough for everyone." He looked at me. "Want me to bring over more steaks? I'll bring some pork chops from the freezer, too. Seems we have just a few unexpected guests for dinner. And I can't wait to hear THAT explanation." He paused slightly, looking at Tristan. "'Your Highness'? This is going to be a good one, I'm sure."

I looked at Nick. "I think that would be a great idea. I have a feeling the stories we are about to hear are going to be incredible. Bring over that head of lettuce and a few tomatoes for salad and more ice, too, so I can make lots of iced tea."

Dinner turned out to be a makeshift event. There were enough steaks and pork chops for everyone but the side dishes varied. No one complained.

Tristan turned to Nick and me. "I think I'll let Togar fill you both in on the entire situation. He can probably do it better than I can."

"Thank you, Sire." Togar bowed his head then looked at us. "It seems obvious to me you have no idea who His Majesty is, so I will try to start at the beginning."

I began pouring more tea as Togar began his tale. He told that Tristan is the only son of the royal family that's been ruling their people for centuries. It had come time for him to take the throne, so his parents could step back. "Yes. Everyone has been waiting for several years for him to take his position as head of the country and his family. Many have watched him grow up and we all know he's going to make an excellent king."

I raised my hand as if I were in a classroom. "I don't mean to interrupt but Tristan is a kind and caring man. He is considerate and helpful. These are qualities I have seen in just the few days he has been here visiting."

Togar continued. "We also realize this. That is how we know he is going to make an excellent ruler. I also believe his encounter with you both was an accident as we don't contact the outside world. We observe it but we try very hard not to interact with it. I do hope His Highness has not told you too much about our world. We cannot let your world know we exist."

Nick jumped in. "Togar. I'll tell you. If our world has not discovered yours by now, they never will. And anyone who thinks they have seen anyone from it and told their story, they'd be laughed out of the room. Folks would wonder what they'd been smoking. For sure."

Togar gave a questioning look. "Smoking?"

"Yes. If they were on some hallucinogenic drug."

A big smile filled Togar's face. "Oh. Yes. I see."

Nick couldn't resist. "Okay. I have to ask. I know you're going to kill us anyway, so I have to know. Your world. Are you from outer space? Are you aliens from another planet?"

Tristan interrupted. "No, Nick. We're not from outer space, aliens from another planet. We are actually aliens from inner space. This planet. Although, our ancestors… but that was in the distant past." He shook his head. "And. No. We're not going to kill you."

This made everyone snicker.

Nick stood up and clapped his hands together and cried out. "WOW! Really? You are from the underworld. Wow! This is totally awesome! Wow! Can you tell us where it is? I mean. Is it under the US or Mexico?"

Tristan smiled. "No. It's out there." He pointed out to sea.

Nick got a big grin on his face and looked at me. "Mu! They're from Mu! The fabled mythical continent of Mu. It was supposedly out in the Pacific and sank thousands of years ago."

Togar spoke up. "Well. Not quite. We have always lived beneath the sea and within the planet. There are enormous cavities in the earth, beneath the sea. Our domed cities on the bottom of the ocean are protected with devices to hide them. But it's not a big deal because the people on the surface know so little about the seas and what's under them. You know more about the stars than you do your own oceans."

Nick shook his head. "You are so right. So right! And no wonder you all travel in submarines." He looked at Togar. "Is yours yellow?" Nick started laughing.

Tristan and I joined in the laughter but Togar couldn't find the humor.

Tristan started singing. "The Beatles. 'We all live in a yellow submarine.... a yellow submarine.... a yellow submarine.'"

At that, everyone began to roar with laughter.

Togar turned to Tristan. "I see your new friend has a very good sense of humor."

Tristan smiled. "Yes. Yes, he does."

Tristan looked at Nick and me. "In case you are wondering how we all know English so well, it's because we are constantly aware of what is happening on the surface. And since the English language became virtually the dominant language across the globe, we have all learned it quite well. It's like so many of you take a foreign language in high school but may never visit the country of that language."

Everyone gave smiles and nods.

After a short pause, Togar turned to Tristan. "Sire. If I might ask. What has made you desire to come here and avoid detection?"

"I needed to think. I needed time to ponder and sort things out. I believe the Fates have worked a miracle bringing me here. I have come to understand something that has been bothering me for a very long time. With the help of these two men, I have come to understand and see."

"But, Sire. I don't understand. How is it you could not resolve your issues at home? I'm sure there are those you could have turned to and resolve any issue or problem."

"Togar. You are wrong. It is a deeply personal issue. But thank you for your concern."

"Sire. If I may speak freely. And I will not say anything that all are not aware of."

"Togar. You've been like a big brother to me throughout my life. You've been with me through thick and thin but this is an issue I couldn't even discuss with you. That's how personal it is."

"Sire. Please, if I may."

"Togar. The floor is yours." Tristan gestured with his hand.

"I believe I know your issue. So. What I'm about to tell you is very, very personal and I will try most desperately to use the right words to explain. Sire. You are the last man on the planet I would do anything to hurt or embarrass in any way. You are dear, not to just me but to all your men here and your people. And your parents most of all."

"I have watched you for many years. I have seen how you react in certain situations and to certain events. One thing that has become very clear is..." Togar looked down toward the floor, cleared his throat then back at Tristan. "Sire. You have never gone on any extended visits or parties with..." He paused again for a moment. "With. With women." He paused for a moment. "Your Majesty. I have seen. You have never been attracted to women. I know you are attracted to... To men." Togar let out a loud sigh. "There. It is said."

There was a long silence before anyone spoke.

Tristan looked at Togar and spoke quietly. "Why have you never come to me before and said anything?"

"Because, Sire, it was not really my place. We thought you would find your own way. We had no idea it was so difficult."

There was silence again.

I spoke softly. "Togar. I must tell you. Dealing with this issue is extremely difficult. In the beginning, you realize you don't have the same connections like other guys do. With girls. You become very confused and you do not understand why. Not that you don't like girls but there just isn't that physical attraction for them. Then, you wonder if you are the only one who is like this. So, you start to immerse yourself in other things, trying to dismiss the confusion."

"Then, you find yourself, being attracted to men and that really throws a wrench into the mix. Because you then try to hide it. You definitely don't want anyone seeing you when you are looking at other men like most men look at women. Yes. It is terrible. But finally, you have to give in and realize you are NOT like other guys. So, you go to where no one knows you and try to live your life. The life you know you are in. Do you know how many young people have committed suicide over this? It is tragic."

"Now, knowing who Tristan truly is and his dilemma, I can't

even begin to imagine the stress in his mind. He is constantly under the spotlight and scrutinized every moment. No wonder he has been alone his whole life. He is not like the average guy who could just go off to somewhere else and live. He is the future ruler of a country. That is incredibly sad. Incredibly sad. He is a fine man and deserves to have a life. Even if he is the king of your world, he deserves his life. He deserves love."

There were a few moments of silence then Nick jumped up. "Everyone deserves love! I don't care who he or she is. They deserve to have it. So, what if he is the king of Mu? That doesn't mean he has to be alone just because he is not like others."

There were a few more moments of quiet before Togar smiled and spoke. "I could not have put it better myself." He began to clap.

Everyone smiled and clapped. The men cried out. "Hear!... Hear!...... Hear!... Hear!"

Tristan smiled. "Wow. It's like a ton of stone has been lifted from my shoulders. Wow! I had no idea everyone knew and it seems not to be an issue with them. Wow. Now, I can go back and be myself and not have to worry."

Nick spoke up. "Yep! You can be yourself and focus on important matters. Oh. And if you're interested in having children, I am sure your people know just how to make that happen. Something tells me your science is far more advanced than ours here on the surface." He shook his head and a questioning look came over his face. "Okay. Just for grins, how long have you all been down there? Under the ocean, I mean."

Tristan turned to Nick. "Our ancestors arrived many thousands of years ago." He pointed at the sky. "From out there. Their sun was about to nova and they had to leave. They are now scattered throughout the universe on worlds with lots of water. We are well suited for the water." He held out his hand with spread fingers and lifted up his foot, making everyone chuckle. "We knew of this planet long before as our scientists were searching for places for everyone to go before catastrophe hit. They discovered many planets that were habitable. One group came here and settled but we don't keep in contact with any of the others. We knew it was too dangerous. It could mean we would be discovered. We took oaths never to interfere with the normal progression of the surface life."

Nick clapped his hands together and cried out. "I love it! I love it!" Then, he looked around. "Are you sure you aren't going to kill us?"

The whole company roared with laughter.

Togar smiled. "Not to worry. We have fixed that. When you wake up tomorrow morning, you will not remember any of us. You will not remember Tristan. You will not remember any of this happening right now. That is why we don't have to kill you. I'm sorry it has to be that way but it must."

Nick shook his head. "Now. How are you going to have that happen? Sounds like you're going to slip something in the tea when we aren't looking."

Togar looked at Nick. "My friend. That is exactly how. And it has already happened."

"But I would never have told anyone. I swear." Nick was adamant.

"That may be true but we could not take the chance."

I turned to Tristan. "Tristan. I care. I care for you more than words can say. But I understand. We are from two different worlds, two different cultures and there could be difficulties. I do understand. Promise me you will go find someone very special there and share your love with him. You have so much to give and you deserve it. I want that for you." I smiled as tears ran down my face. "All I ask is you hug me one last time before I don't remember you." I stood up and walked toward Tristan.

Tristan stood and we hugged tightly. We then sat down.

Togar shook his head. He spoke softly. "Sire. I am so sorry. It is obvious, this man is not just any man to you. You have a connection with him. I wish there was some way. I don't know what to say."

Tristan spoke softly. "Togar. You're right. I wish there was a way. I want there to be a way."

Nick spoke up. "Damn. This is like the scene out of the movie, 'Roman Holiday'. Geez."

I looked over to Tristan, smiled and tears continued to run down my face. "Tristan. I understand. You and I are two but there are many who need you. If this is the way it must be, then so be it. Togar says I will never remember you. My heart will always remember you. I hope you will remember me. I love you, Tristan."

Tristan came over and grabbed me, holding me close. I heard him whisper. "I love you so much, you silly goose." At that, I fell asleep in his arms.

CHAPTER XIV

I awoke and could see it was a new day just beginning. Sitting up, I stretched my arms up in the air. I was rather shocked at myself. I knew I was tired from the trip down from Atlanta. But when I got here, I sure as hell didn't expect my little nap to last till the next morning. I wondered what I was going to do today. It was the first full day of my vacation and I was going to enjoy it.

Getting out of bed, I dressed to go to the kitchen and fix breakfast. I opened the bedroom door. That's when I smelled a hint of turpentine. "What can that be? Did somehow one of my bottles of turpentine get broken?" I sniffed the air and walked into the living room. I stopped and stared at the wall. There was a painting of a sunset. "Wow. Where the hell did that come from?" I walked over and examined the picture. It was one of mine. "When the hell did I paint that? And it's still wet."

Just then, I heard a noise on the terrace. I turned and looked out. There was Nick, slowly coming across toward the door. I shook my head. "When the hell did you get here? And how? You weren't supposed to be coming till the end of the week."

Nick walked in and saw me staring at him. He looked at me with major questioning on his face. "Okay. I give up. How the hell did I get here? And I swear. I have NOT done any drugs."

I looked at him with surprise. "I swear. I am totally, totally confused. I was going to ask you the same thing but if you don't know, I think we need to talk. You were not coming till Thursday at the earliest because of your project." Then, I pointed at the painting. "Do you see a painting over there? A sunset painting?"

Nick looked and answered. "Ah. Yes. Yes. I do."

"Well. Thank, God. I'm not imagining it. You're not going to believe this. I know I did it but I have no idea when." I looked directly at Nick. "And this is supposed to be my first day here. What the hell is going on?"

Nick shook his head. "Okay. This is very scary. The last thing I remember before I got out of bed a few minutes ago, is getting on the plane to come here. I'm pretty sure I called you to let you know I was coming."

"Let's have a cup and go over this. I swear. If you did call, I don't remember talking with you." We went into the kitchen, made a cup of coffee and went out onto the terrace.

Nick spoke. "I guess the first question is this. What day is it? You think it's Sunday. Your first full day of vacation but I didn't leave until the Wednesday night after you were here already. So. For me, this would be Thursday. Yeah. Something is so wrong here." He paused for a moment and looked at the ground. "Just a second. The clock in my bedroom has the time and date on it."

Nick jumped up and ran to his house. Shortly, he returned. "It's Friday. Friday, May the fifteenth."

"What!? What?? It's Sunday, May the third. Are you sure?" I yelled out. "How can that be. This is crazy. I just got here. And that was on Saturday, May the second. But if it's not May the third. Oh. Wow. What has happened? I'm missing virtually two weeks. Holy shit!"

"Okay! Okay! Try to remember. Try to remember anything. You have been here for almost two damn weeks. You have to remember something!" Nick was firm. "Just a second. Let's check. Look around. Is there anything different than you remember?"

Nick and I got up and slowly walked around the living room then came back out on the terrace.

"The only thing I can see is the painting on the wall. How about your house?"

We ran over and checked. There was nothing out of the ordinary there, so we returned to my terrace and sat down.

"I have to admit. This really has me concerned." Nick shook his head. "I have never had a memory lapse like this before. Geez. This is crazy. You've lost two weeks and I've lost one."

"I know this is going to sound like the last thing we need but I need a drink." I shook my head.

Nick threw his hands in the air. "You know. I agree. Since you've been here for two weeks already, check and see if you have any of your great Bloody Marys already made up. I sure could use one right now."

I went in, checking the fridge. Yep. There was a container, so I fixed us both one. I handed Nick one as I sat down again. "Just give me a few. Maybe I can remember something." Quietly, I sat there concentrating.

Nick shook his head and patted his stomach. "Well. I have to say. It is obvious I have not missed any meals in a week."

My mouth twisted. "How could we have been here the length of time we have and not be able to remember a thing? Seriously. I have no recollection of coming to get you at the airport but that's what had to have happened for you to be here. Or did you rent a car?"

Nick jumped up with his hands on his hips and yelled. "I wonder." He immediately ran off the terrace toward his house.

I yelled. "Where are you going?"

"To possibly save our sanity."

Some ten minutes went by when he came running back and sat down. In his hand was a notebook. "I haven't looked yet but this just might be our memory."

I jerked my head. "I don't understand. What is that?"

"It's my notebook journal. I write things down in it if I find them interesting or want to remember them. Not quite a daily diary but close. If there's anything in here, I want you to be here with me when I read it, so we both will have a clue." Nick opened the book and slowly turned the pages as he peered down at them. Suddenly, he stopped.

"Ah." He was silent for a moment then spoke softly. "Oh, my God. Oh, my God. Here it is. I DID call you and I wrote here that you've met someone."

"WHAT!!?? I yelled out. "What!? I met someone!? Who the hell could that be?"

"Yep. And you were going to explain when I got here." He started reading aloud but in a mumble fashion running over the words. "Oh. Wow! Are you ready? His name. His name is Tristan. Holy shit! And he has deformed hands and feet."

"What? Deformed hands and feet?"

"It says here 'they are webbed and his feet look kinda like flippers'."

"Nick! Are you pulling some kind of joke? This is ridiculous."

"No. 'He came out of the sea on a raft.' Just a sec." He mumbled some more. "He seems to be from a wealthy family." He paused, reading silently for a few seconds then looked at me and smiled. "And you really like him. I mean. You REALLY like him. And he is a totally cool guy. Just your type. Big, tall, dark fur all over. And it says 'he has such intense blue eyes'. The kind that 'can see your soul'. Wow." He kept reading. Then, he yelled out. "And he is just like you! And from what I have down here, 'he really likes you as well'."

"Okay. How is it I can really like someone and not remember him? What has happened?" I pounded my right fist on the table.

"Wait a minute. I wrote here 'the portrait of him is an amazing likeness'." He looked at me. "What portrait? I don't see any portrait, hanging in the living room. Where else could it be?"

I stood up. "Come with me. Maybe I know." We headed to the first guest bedroom. Nothing but a well-made bed was there. We opened the door to the second guest bedroom. There across the room was an easel, holding a covered canvas.

"Let me see. I don't remember setting this up." I carefully

removed the cloth, covering the canvas, revealing a very well-done portrait.

My mouth fell open. "Oh, my God! How in blue blazes have I forgotten a man like that? I don't care if he does have webbed hands and flipper feet. I have to be insane."

"From what I wrote about him, that's him all right. That... is Tristan."

I grabbed the canvas off the easel and we headed back to the terrace. I leaned the painting up against the wall, so the breeze wouldn't knock it over. We sat down.

Nick kept reading in his notebook. "There was an earthquake. Last Friday." Nick looked up and pounded his fist on the table. "An earthquake. My very first earthquake! And I don't remember it! That sucks!" He shook his head then looked back down at the book and kept reading. "Says Tristan went out to check his..." He paused for a moment. "Hot damn! You are NOT going to believe this. He has a submarine. He went to check to make sure his submarine was all right after the quake. We kidded him, asking if it was yellow." Nick started to giggle and began singing. "'We all live in a yellow submarine... a yellow submarine... a yellow submarine... We all live...'"

"Okay! Okay! We get it!" I shouted. "Sorry, Nick. I just am so edgy over this whole thing. But you have to be kidding. He has a submarine?"

"Well. We never saw it. Or at least, I have no mention of us ever seeing it. What can I say?" He kept reading in a mumbling manner then finally stopped. "The last thing I wrote was on Wednesday. This past Wednesday. Everything seemed to be going fine. I have nothing written here to indicate any trouble or problems. Whatever happened to us, happened yesterday as I have no entry for yesterday at all. Nothing. Nada." He closed the notebook and set it on the table.

Nick spoke quietly. "I think we need to just relax and try to think this through. Let's fix something to eat and then just chill for a while."

"I think you're right. I'll fix us an omelet. How's that?" I stood up and headed to the kitchen.

"Sounds good to me. Need any help?"

"Nope. But if you'd pour us another Bloody, I'd appreciate it."

As we sat and ate breakfast, then it hit me. I gasped almost choking on the food in my mouth. I started coughing.

Nick jumped up and slapped me on the back several times. "What's wrong? Are you all right?"

"It just dawned on me. I'm supposed to fly home tomorrow. But I tell you right now. That's not going to happen till we get this thing figured out to some extent."

I called the airline and canceled my flight. I was not going to book another one yet. I also called work and told them I was going to be delayed for some time due to a personal issue. They understood and told me to take as much time as I needed. Nick did the same.

All day we sat looking at the painting of Tristan, trying to remember anything. It was useless. Neither of us could come up with anything.

Finally, it was time to hit the hay. Maybe the next day would be more productive.

Over the next few days, Nick and I tried to recall anything we could about the missing days and our encounter with Tristan. Where did he go? Maybe he was some spy for some foreign country. We dismissed that due to his hands and feet. Other than that, neither of us could come up with anything. That's when we decided it was time to go home. Since the painting was still wet, I left it on the easel. I covered it again to keep any dust getting in the wet paint.

Going back to work helped some for both of us. Nick immersed himself in getting the big project off the ground that was to begin in mid-June. For me, my work kept me busy but I continued trying to remember the missing time in Mexico.

Then, one night I woke up quickly and sat up in bed. It was a dream. I quickly got up and ran down the hall to Nick's room and knocked on the door. "Nick. Are you awake?"

A groggy voice came from the other side of the door. "I am now. What is it?"

"I had a dream."

"A dream?"

"Yes. About Tristan."

There was a fumbling noise and the door quickly opened. Nick stared at me with blurry eyes. "Really!? You remembered something? Tell me."

I went into his room and we both sat on the bed. I told him what I could remember of the dream. Every description I could remember, I told to Nick. I was so happy in the dream. We were so close. I could feel his touch, his warmth, his caring. I could feel the love I had for him.

Nick shook his head. "That was no dream. You were remembering. I think that's a good thing." He looked at me and smiled. "From what I had written in my notebook, you both cared a great deal for one another. Now. Let's go have a cup and then go back to bed."

It was maybe two weeks later I was woken by a knock at my door. It was Nick. "I just had a dream. We need to sit down for this one."

"What? Nick. Here, sit on the bed. Tell me what you remember."

"I can only remember a small piece but it's very disturbing."

"Okay. I'm ready. Tell me."

"We are sitting on your terrace. Down there. There are three of us. You, me and Tristan. We are having a fun time when all of a sudden, I turn and from out of the ocean I see a bunch of guys and they are coming up to the house. Now. Are you ready for this? They come up to the terrace, stand in formation, hit their chests with their fists then go down on their right knee. The guy, who seems to be the leader of the pack, looks up at Tristan and says 'Your Highness'. Yeah. They called Tristan, 'Your Highness'. And one other thing I remember. They had feet and hands like Tristan."

"Really? 'Your Highness'? Holy crap! He is royalty of some sort? This is too crazy. This whole thing sounds like some grade 'B' movie. Is it possible we ate something in Mexico that has done this to us?"

"Hey. Maybe that's why we can't remember. Maybe we weren't supposed to remember. Maybe they hypnotized us, so we would forget."

I shook my head. "I don't think that's possible. You can't make people forget two weeks of their life. I can't imagine that happening. But as my mother tells me, never say never. Who knows?"

Nick responded. "Since they all had feet and hands alike, maybe they were from some colony we have never heard of. But you would think something like that would be all over the news." Nick paused for a moment. "You know. Maybe someone gave us some really powerful drugs or acid. Hey. Stuff like that crap can make you see flying elephants and you'd swear they were real. So, I've been told."

"Well. I have to admit. That is very interesting. And you can't remember anything else?"

Nick shrugged his shoulders. "Sorry. But the 'Your Highness' shocked me right out of a dead sleep."

For the next two months, both of us were having dreams, remembering bits and pieces of the time with Tristan. I came to know and understand I had fallen in love with him. It didn't matter if he was royalty. I still couldn't stop my feelings for him. The one thing we couldn't remember is what happened after Nick's revelation or where they all went. Slowly, we began to put the time puzzle together. But huge pieces were missing.

September came and I couldn't take it any longer. I had to get back to Mexico. I told Nick of my plan and he wanted to go as well since his big project had been completed and there was a lull in his workload. He said we had been together through thick and thin. We were not going to leave each other now. And so, off we flew.

We rented a car and as normal, we stopped at the grocery store to stock up before heading to the house.

Our first night there was uneventful. We cooked on the grill and had drinks on the terrace. It was funny but we both agreed we felt better being there. There was a comfort for some unknown reason.

We were sitting quietly when Nick said he was going to turn on the radio.

I commented. "You do know all we're going to hear is some Cucaracha music?"

He smiled. "That's okay. Do you mind?"

"Oh, why not."

Strangely, the station he turned to was playing an old song in English. The next several songs were ones that had been hits in the states years ago. I was surprised to hear it.

Several songs played. Then, came one that had a single note, pensive entry beat that caught my attention. Suddenly, the performer began to sing. I instantly recognized who it was. I loved Roy Orbison's music. I got up quickly and ran over to the radio, turning up the volume.

As the song progressed, I realized I had never heard the song before. I thought I had heard every one of Roy Orbison's songs but I now knew, I was wrong.

I stood by the radio and listened. *A Love So Beautiful* filled the air. Every word was so clear and the melody line was haunting. I couldn't believe how incredibly beautiful the song was. But as it progressed, I heard how it was so indescribably sad. I immediately thought of Tristan. The song continued. 'A love so beautiful.... in every way.... A love so beautiful.... we let it slip away.' Tears began streaming down my face. The words were so emotional and powerful. As the song came to an end, I completely lost it and started crying uncontrollably.

Nick jumped up and came over, hugging me.

I cried on his shoulder. "The song is so sad. So sad. I could feel the pain. I had a love so beautiful and now, it's gone. It has slipped away."

After a few minutes, we sat down and I composed myself. "I have never heard that song before in my life. How is that? I thought I had heard every one of Roy Orbison's songs. And this one is so powerful. Geez. Wow. I'm so sorry. I had no idea it was going to hit me this way."

"Not to worry. But you're right. It's a very powerful song and very, very sad. The melody line just magnifies the sadness."

I began wiping the tears from my face. "Damn. I definitely could use a drink now." I looked at Nick.

Nick looked over at me and smiled. "Stay there. I'll get one for both of us."

The next day, we walked on the beach. I thought that might help me remember more. As I looked out to sea, my heart seemed to cry out in pain. I couldn't hold back the tears. It was crazy but I was heartbroken over a person I couldn't even remember meeting except only in dreams. Nick would just pat me on the back, give me a little hug to console me and we would continue our walk.

Every time I looked at the portrait of Tristan, my heart grew even heavier. I could hear Roy Orbison singing his beautiful sad song in my head which immediately brought on a flood of tears. I couldn't explain it, but I knew more and more there was a great connection with the man in the painting. The man I couldn't remember meeting in person. I knew I had lost the great love of my life.

It was late afternoon and we were sitting on the terrace. Nick quietly spoke. "Well. The gypsy lady was right. You found your Destiny all right. Only to lose it. Geez. I could have sworn she said you would find happiness."

I took a sip of my iced tea and grinned. "Well. From what I can put together, I did find happiness. It just wasn't for a very long time."

Nick pounded his right fist into his left palm. "I still think there's more to this. Somehow, the pieces of this puzzle are not coming together correctly. That gypsy lady was not a scammer. She was straight up. Something tells me this isn't over yet. The fat lady has not sung."

I quickly stood up, put my left hand on my chest, the right one up in the air and broke into the great Leoncavallo aria from Pagliacci. I stopped after a few words were sung and looked over at Nick.

Nick shook his head. "Sorry. You're not fat enough."

This had us in almost uncontrollable laughter.

Nick shook his head. "At least we're trying to find some humor in this tragedy." He just smiled. After a moment, he raised his glass of tea. "Hey. You still have me." He gave a big grin.

I raised my glass and gave a big smile. "You're right about that. Friends forever."

Nick called out. "Friends forever."

We touched our glasses together.

CHAPTER XV

It was the next evening, Nick and I were sitting on the terrace, watching the sunset. Nick happened to turn and looked out to sea. "Hey. What's that? Looks like a raft out there beyond the rocks." He pointed.

I turned and looked. Yes. It did look like a raft in the fading light. Several seconds later, it looked like someone was getting into the raft. Finally, it was obvious. It was someone in a raft and he was rowing toward the shore.

"I was right. It's a raft and it's coming this way." Nick stood up and pointed again.

I stood up and whispered. "Could it be? Could it be him?"

"Oh, my God! Maybe it's him!" Nick cried out. "Quick! Let's go down and meet him when he gets ashore." He grabbed my arm and pulled me. We both started walking fast toward the beach. We were some fifteen feet from where the water met the sand and stood and waited.

As the raft got closer, the occupant had to have seen us standing on the shore as he directed the raft in our direction. Entering shallower water, he got out and pulled the raft behind him. Shortly, he was standing some eight feet from us. He let go of the raft and stood silent.

Even in the dim light, I could see his face was that of the portrait in the house. It was Tristan. I looked into his eyes and spoke softly. "Tristan. It's you."

Tristan looked at me strangely with surprise. "I don't understand. How do you know me? You should not be able to remember me." He looked at Nick. "And it should be the same for you. No one has ever been able to resist the drug Togar gave you both."

Nick just smiled. "Love is a powerful thing, ain't it? Powerful thing!"

Tristan shook his head. "It sure is. It sure is. It's one reason I'm standing here right now."

Nick jumped in again. "Okay. Instead of standing here on the beach, let's all go up to the house and talk. Something tells me there is much to be said."

Tristan grabbed one side of his raft and Nick grabbed the other side and we all headed up to the terrace. When we arrived, I asked if anyone would like some iced tea. Hands were raised.

Sitting around the table on the terrace, the conversation began with Tristan. "I have waited for you to return. I just knew you would but was not sure when. But how is it you have any memory of me?"

"Memory of you? How about memory of you and several others. And one of them calling you 'Your Highness'." Nick blurted out.

Tristan looked at Nick with surprise. "No way? Really? But how?"

"Well." Nick smiled. "It actually started, during our last visit here back in May. We were both so confused because of the lost time we couldn't account for or remember. Fortunately enough, I keep a little journal notebook."

A questioning look came to Tristan's face. "I thought we had wiped all evidence of us being here."

"There was no way you knew of my notebook. It's something I'd never mentioned. And another thing. You were unaware of the painting."

"But I did know of the painting. The sunset. It's hanging in the living room." Tristan turned in the direction of the living room.

"Oh. No. Not the sunset. The other painting." Nick gave a big grin. "After I read the passages in my journal and saw the painting, bits and pieces of the mysterious puzzle began to come together.

Then, when we returned home, that's when the dreams started. Slowly, more of forgotten memories began to return. What made us realize the dreams were more than dreams is because they came to both of us."

I looked at Tristan and smiled. "That's when it became so obvious to me and I realized, I was in love with someone I didn't ever remember meeting in person. He was only a phantom of my dreams. But he was so real. And I knew exactly what you looked like because the painting confirmed it. As Nick said, we were both having similar dreams and we knew that couldn't possibly happen if there wasn't some truth to them. Finally, I knew I had to come back here and see if I could understand more. Maybe things would make more sense here and maybe we could remember more here."

"But how could you know what I looked like? I do not understand." Tristan shook his head.

Nick spoke up again. "The painting. It did not lie." He stood up. "Come. Let me show you." He turned to me. "You don't mind, do you?"

I gestured with my hands. "The floor is yours."

We all stood and Nick led the way to the guest bedroom. He opened the door, turned on the light and pointed to the easel and the covered canvas sitting on it, standing across the room. "That painting."

I walked over and removed the cloth. I turned and looked at Tristan.

Tristan's face was filled with surprise. Then, it changed. His eyes filled with tears and they began streaming down his face. After a few moments, he took a breath and spoke softly with a shaking in his voice. "Oh, my God. It's amazing. But when? You had to be doing it when I was here. But you never told me."

I smiled at him. "Yes. I had to have been painting it at the same time I was doing the sunset. Yes. When you were here. That's how I knew what you looked like. It also answered the question as to the man in my dreams."

"I guess Togar never thought to look in this room or under the cloth as I told him we had never come into this room."

Nick clapped his hands. "Destiny and the Fates. They work in strange and mysterious ways. What can I say?"

We headed back to the terrace and sat down. Nick continued. "But what are you doing here and how did you know we were here? 'Enquiring minds want to know.'"

Tristan looked at the floor and shook his head. Then, he looked at us both. "After Togar and his men put you both to bed that night, we quickly tried to erase all evidence of us ever being here. The one thing we knew we couldn't change was the loss of time. We had no idea about the notebook or the portrait painting. What can I say?"

"Some of Togar's men brought my sub home and I rode with Togar. I will tell you. Togar was constantly apologizing for doing what was done but he knew that contact with the surface world was absolutely forbidden even though he saw how I was emotionally connected to you. All the way home, we talked. Now, he understands."

"You should have seen my parents when I got home. At first, they were furious. Especially, my father. But very soon afterward, they saw how I was. They began to understand. Over several months, we talked and talked and talked. They finally got it. Togar even came to me and said I should go with my heart."

I looked at Tristan and gasped. "That is exactly what the old gypsy lady told me. Wow."

Tristan continued. "That's when I told them. Whatever the repercussions, I was coming back for you. I was going to tell you I can't live without you. You are my heart and I cannot live without my heart. And I could only hope that in time, you would remember me and see how much I love you. I was hoping you would come back with me and live with me as my partner. I hoped in time, you might care for and love me just half as much as I do for you."

We both stood up and walked to one another and hugged.

Tristan continued. "I had no idea you would know me. I'm still in shock that you know and remember me. And you truly do love me. It's amazing."

Nick grinned. "Okay. I hate to break up this lovey-dovey but 'enquiring minds' are not satisfied yet. How did you know we were here?"

"I knew you would be returning one day, so I came back here and placed a device to detect your presence. That's how I knew you were here." He got up and walked into the dining area and reached under the table, removing a small square object. He held it in the air as he returned and sat down.

"Totally cool!" Nick smiled. "Chicka Boom! Chicka Boom! Don't ya jest luv it?" He clapped his hands together and yelled. "YeeeHaw!!" After a bit of laughing, he commented. "Okay. I have a suggestion. I'm hungry. I don't know about you all but I have to eat something."

I jumped up. "Geez. Yes. Let's fix some burgers on the grill. I have a feeling you haven't eaten all day." I looked at Tristan.

Tristan smiled. "I would love a hamburger."

Conversation continued as we cooked and ate. Tristan was still in shock that Nick's and my memories had not been fully erased. "Yes. Togar is going to be very surprised."

After we finished eating, Whiskey Sours were poured all around. We couldn't stop putting puzzle pieces together.

Tristan turned to me. "Well. What do you think about the idea? It will be the first time an outsider has come to live with us."

Nick yelled out. "Hey! The gypsy lady was right." He looked at me. "And if you don't go, you won't be fulfilling your Destiny like she said."

"I want to go so much but what about all this? What about my job, my obligations?"

Nick looked hard at me. "Sign a paper and turn everything over to me. I'll take care of it. Don't worry. Your house will still be here if you both ever want to come and get away for a while. I'll make sure nothing happens to it."

I questioned. "But how are you going to explain where I went? Even a note with my signature on it is going to raise major red flags."

"Not to worry. I'll come up with something." Nick paused for a moment then broke out in loud laughter. "I have it! I can say you were abducted... by aliens!"

We all joined the laughter.

CHAPTER XVI

The next day, Nick and I went into town and found our old real estate agent to see if she knew of a good lawyer. It was no problem as she had to deal with them with her real estate business. We went and filled out paperwork to make everything legal, so it would reduce major questions. All papers were signed and notarized.

I also called my boss and told him a major event had occurred in my life and I wouldn't be able to come back to work. He was sad I was leaving but understood and wished me well.

Returning to the house, I began to get the things I wanted to take with me. I realized I didn't need to take much as I was sure anything I needed would be available where I was going. One thing I did do was go under the stairs and get a really nice frame for Tristan's portrait. That was going with me since it was dry. Tristan said he had a very large bag that would seal to get it down to the sub. He was right. It didn't get wet or damaged at all getting there. It's what we used to bring all the things I wanted to take with me down to the sub.

He had also brought an air tank with mouthpiece and hose, so I could get down to the sub as well. It was in hopes I would go with him. He made me practice several times with it to make sure I felt comfortable using it.

It was the next day all was ready. Everything I was taking with me was in the sub. We three stood on the beach.

Nick looked at me and smiled. "Remember? The old gypsy

lady told me that one day I was going to have to let you go. Well. I think this is the day." He grabbed me and hugged me tightly. "I will miss you, my friend, but I know you're going to be happy. That's what's important. And above all things, I wish you happiness." He turned to Tristan. "Good buddy, I know you will love and make him happy. You would never have returned if you didn't have strong and powerful feelings for him. I wish you both all the happiness you deserve." He grabbed Tristan, hugging him. "Take good care of my brother."

I looked at Nick. "I will always remember and love you. And even though we're not related, you will always be my brother, too. And who knows? Maybe our paths will cross again one day."

Tristan and I got in the raft. Tristan took the oar and began rowing out to sea. As I watched Nick get farther and farther away from me, I could only hear Madame Zelda in my head. "Your Destiny and happiness are in the sea." I smiled, realizing she was right.

I strapped on the air tank and put the mouthpiece in my mouth. I looked to the shore. Nick was still standing there. I could tell he was smiling as he waved his right arm in the air. I raised my right arm up and waved back. After a few moments, I leaned back into the water. My new life was beginning.

It was June, two thousand. It was the year Nick and I had planned on coming to Mexico to celebrate our fortieth birthday. Tristan thought it a terrific idea to come back to the house and see if he might be there and have a fun birthday celebration.

It was mid-June when we reached the place. It was the exact time Nick and I had discussed coming. Tristan got the raft ready and brought it to the surface. Next, I readied and went up. We both climbed into the raft. Tristan started rowing toward shore.

It was the middle of the afternoon as we approached the beach. I was looking up to Nick's house. Suddenly, I saw him come running from the house, waving his arms in the air and yelling out. "You came!!! You came!!!"

As Tristan and I got closer to shore, Nick came running out into the water to meet us. We jumped out of the raft and started pulling it to shore. Nick was there in a shot. He grabbed me and hugged me tightly. "You came! I wasn't sure you'd remember. It's so good to see you." He turned to Tristan. "Good to see you, big guy. I see you have been taking very good care of my buddy. Don't think I have ever seen him look so happy." He grabbed one side of the raft to help Tristan pull it up to the house. We headed to Nick's terrace.

Getting to the terrace, Nick told us to sit down. He was going to get us all drinks. He also pulled several steaks out of the freezer for dinner. After serving the drinks, he ran back into the house again. Shortly, he returned carrying a cake. A big grin filled his face and he cried out. "HAPPY BIRTHDAY!" He placed the cake on the table.

I looked at it and read out loud what was written on it. "Happy Birthday to Us!" I almost started to cry. I went over and gave Nick a big hug. "Has anyone told you lately what an amazing friend you are?"

We all sat down at the table.

Nick smiled. "Okay! I have to know. 'Enquiring minds' need to know. What is it like? I can't wait to hear all about it. How are the folks feeling about you?" He looked at me with a huge grin.

"Nick. It's amazing. Madame Zelda was so right. I can't begin to explain how happy I am. Everyone there is so accepting of me and they all are happy for Tristan. I must tell you. Living down there is very different than up here."

"Wow. I'll bet it's amazing. You must tell me more later but first I have to say this." He stood up and lifted his glass. "To an incredible friend. Knowing you are happy makes me so glad. And... Happy Birthday!"

Tristan and I stood up and raised our glasses. They all clinked together. We all called out. "HAPPY BIRTHDAY!"

Nick turned to Tristan. "Here's to you, big guy, for making my most amazing friend happy. I will thank you for that for the rest of my days."

All glasses clinked together again.

I looked at Nick. "And here's to a friend I have had forever. We are friends forever."

The glasses rang out again.

I turned to Tristan. "To a man who has made me happy and loved more than I could have ever imagined. I love you so much."

The glasses rang again.

Tristan looked at Nick and then at me. "And a very Happy Fortieth Birthday to you both. I consider myself so lucky to have you as a friend." He smiled at Nick then turned to me. "And I thank the Fates every day for leading me to you. You have given me more love and happiness than I could have ever imagined. I love you so much. Happy Birthday to you both."

We touched the glasses together again.

I raised my left hand in the air. "There's one more to remember." I paused for a few seconds and glanced up into the air. "To Madame Zelda. If not for her and the things she said, this may never have happened." I raised my glass. "To Madame Zelda."

All the glasses touched and rang out as we all called out. "Hear!... Hear!...... Hear!... Hear!"

Nick looked at Tristan. "I want to be honest with you. I swear. I swear I have never said the first word about you or about Mu. I made that promise and I have kept it." He raised his glass. "There was no way I would betray my best friend and the one he loves."

Tristan smiled. "Thank you, Nick. You really are a true friend."

I looked at Nick and smiled. "Yes, you are."

For the next few hours, I began to tell Nick of the world below and how incredible it is. We chatted through dinner. After eating, we all sat back again for a bit more talking before hitting the hay.

Nick said he had made sure the bed in my house was fresh, hoping I might show up.

Finally, the conversation got to where I wanted. It was something Tristan and I had discussed numerous times over the last many months.

"Nick. I wanted to bring something up. Tristan and I have talked about it many times. There is a position Tristan wants filled. An engineering position. Talking to me about it, he asked me the kind of qualifications you had." I paused for a moment shaking my head. "I didn't think Tristan was serious but he was dead serious."

Nick looked at me and then at Tristan. "Really? You're kidding me. Really? No way?"

Tristan smiled. "Yep. I am serious. There would be only one catch. You would have to leave the surface and stay down with us."

Nick clapped both his hands together. "Wow! Amazing! From the moment I saw you had come here, do you know I have wanted to ask you if you needed someone like me down there to help out. But wasn't quite sure how to approach it. I didn't want to intrude. I mean, things up here are fine but I've really missed our friendship." Nick smiled at me. "And I've definitely missed your cooking. Tristan. Have you tasted his fried chicken? Holy cow. I love it. Do you have fried chicken down there?"

We all broke into raucous laughter.

I was totally taken aback. "You mean you really would consider it?"

"Hell yeah! I would love to go! I'd just have to clear up a few things here. Well. I mean on the surface. We could go in and get that same lawyer we did before and I can put everything in my sister's name and turn it all over to her. Some time ago, I hired a guy to assist me with my position at work, so giving him the whole kit-n-kaboodle wouldn't be a problem. Wow! I can't believe you both want me to come down there. Wow. YeeeHaw!!!"

Tristan smiled. "Well. You both were supposed to be friends forever and this way it can happen. The palace has a ton of space and room. We can set you up in one of the apartments right next to our quarters. It would virtually be like it was here, living next door to one another. Nick. You're a great guy and it would be terrific if you'd come back with us after this birthday visit."

Nick yelled out. "GROUP HUG!!!"

We all stood and hugged each other.

Then, Nick flexed his eyebrows several times. "Okay. What are the girls like there?"

We all cracked up again and toasted with our drinks.

The next day, Nick and I went into town and met with the lawyer. He was extremely helpful in making sure all was in order for the transfer of property and other assets to Nick's sister.

Nick commented. "I would really like to take the paintings you gave me that are hanging on the walls in my house. So, I could put them in my new living space in Mu. What do you think?"

I giggled. "Funny you should say that. I'm getting all the ones in my house, too. Tristan brought that big bag again, so we could get stuff down to the sub."

Nick called his sister. "Hey, Barbara. Nick here. Yeah. It's been a while, I know. Listen. I'm calling you to let you know. I'm transferring everything over to you. You'll be getting copies of stuff in about a month or so. Probably longer as the mail is not the speediest here. Yes. I'm in Mexico. The paperwork will explain everything. Why? Well. I'm going away. No. I'm not dying. Yes. It is necessary as it is a new job, far, far away...... and I most likely won't ever be back. As I said, I'm in Mexico right now but will be leaving in the next day or so. I'm also taking the paintings from both the houses here. So, don't think they were stolen. I wanted to let you know and to tell you goodbye. Oh, no. It's a fantastic job and I just cannot turn it down. Believe me. It's the kind of job any engineer would give his eye-teeth for. The job of a lifetime. What can I say? So, take care and be happy. Love you. Bye."

The next day, Nick called his assistant. "Robert. Hey. Nick here. Listen. I wanted to let you know I want you to take over my position and if necessary, hire you an assistant. Why? I just got an offer to do an incredible job in a foreign land. I have to leave tomorrow or I'll lose the chance. It's something I've had on my bucket list and I can't believe it's actually happening. I'll most likely never come back here again. Yes. I'm sending paperwork to my sister who will be the one to deal with any of my benefits and such. I have given her all executrix authority. So, she probably will place me as legally dead in seven years. Don't you just love it? Okay, Robert. Listen. You take care and do a good job. The company will love you for it. You bet. Goodbye."

The next day, we finally got everything brought down to the sub. It took a while as Tristan was the one doing it all. That done, we gathered on Nick's terrace and had one last drink.

We all stood as Nick raised his glass in the air. "To the future and a new beginning. A new beginning. Just like Madame Zelda said."

We were all smiling as the three glasses rang out when they touched. We all cheered.

Shortly thereafter, we walked to the beach. Nick and I stopped, turned, looking up and down the beach and lastly at the two houses and smiled.

Nick spoke softly. "I wonder what Madame Zelda would say if she could see us now and realize what was happening?"

I looked up into the air and smiled. "I have a feeling she already knows. Yep. I have a feeling she is smiling like never before."

Nick and I looked at one another and hugged.

We all pushed the raft out into the water and got in. As we paddled out to sea, Nick commented. "Ah. Tristan! One thing. You never did tell me. 'Enquiring minds want to know.'"

Tristan looked at Nick with a questioning expression. "Nick. What's that?"

Nick grinned. "Your submarine. Is it yellow?"

We all just roared with laughter.

As for me, I had everything I wanted. I had an amazing man as my partner who loved me and who I loved more than words could say. And I had my best friend there as well. A friend who had been with me through thick and thin. Just like Madame Zelda had said it, we would truly be..... friends forever.

The End

PostScript

I tried to pull a Daphne du Maurier with this story. Like she did in <u>Rebecca</u>. Did you catch it?

I watched the old movie with Laurence Olivier and Joan Fontaine. After it was over, I was telling someone about it and how terrific it was. I started naming the characters but for the life of me, I could not remember the name of Joan Fontaine's character. I thought that strange.

Not long afterward, I got to watch it again and I paid close attention to see what her name was. Well. If you know what I'm talking about, you already know the answer. There is no name. Joan Fontaine's character never has a name. She is referred to in several ways, like 'my dear', 'sweetheart' or 'my darling' but never by a given name. I thought how clever.

So. Did you catch it? The main character in my story has no name. GRIN!

Printed in the United States
by Baker & Taylor Publisher Services